SHANNON 1
W. BLOOMFIELD

I THANK GOD FOR GIVING ME THE STRENGTH TO FINISH THIS BOOK. IT IS DEDICATED TO AARON MICHAEL & JORDAN ALEXANDER SHANNON,

AND TO ALL THOSE WHO NEVER GAVE UP ON ME & ALWAYS BELIEVED.

MY LOVE, ALWAYS, TO ETHEL & JAMES SHANNON, TARYN G.CARTER & PATRICIA ANN SHANNON.

BLOOMFIELD

BY J.A. Shannon

Chapter I

It was the perfect ending to an incredibly stressful day, or so I thought going into it. The entire day, I was dealing with construction people, city inspectors and a handful of alcohol and food vendors.

My Restaurant and Nightclub, The Playground,

was due to open in a few short days and tons of last minute details were piling

up on my PDA. To make a long story short, when my best friend called and asked me to join him and his girlfriend at a nearby Jazz club, I was out of there.

I left as quickly as I could.

Besides, I was starting to get hungry.

It only took 10 minutes to tool over to the restaurant inside of General Motors World Headquarters, and as I Pulled up to the valet station off the promenade and stopped the car, the valet approached.

"Are you here for dinner Sir?"

Upon receiving a positive answer that I was heading into Seldom Blues he handed me a cream-colored ticket stub, then placed another on the windshield of my car. I handed him the keys and he slipped behind the wheel of my midnight blue Maserati Granturismo. Carefully driving off to park it within the building's parking lot catacombs.

My friend Paul and his girlfriend Sophie were already there, with a chilled bottle of Champagne on the table.

Paul was a real estate investor who owned several houses. We also had several business ventures together, including a loft apartment building that we were opening soon.

He was dressed for the occasion in a black pinstriped Armani suit and tie. His short dreads, neatly lined around his head, while Sophie's red hair, locked and curly, flowed nearly to her shoulders and fell on the black dress she wore.

Sophie was a neo-soul type of singer. Preparing to release her very first full length CD, independently.
From the songs that I heard, the album was going to be a collection of soothing Jazz and R&B. Upbeat with an old soul flavor, and I couldn't wait for it to be finished.
They had just returned from the studio and were using tonight as an excuse of celebrating that she only had five more songs to go. Paul and Sophie never needed an excuse to celebrate, but it was interesting to hear some of the excuses they made up.
I think it was one of the first things that made us all friends.
" Damn, dog, is the car and sidewalk still in one piece", Paul joked. "You got here quick as hell."
" What it do, Core", said Sophie.
"What can I say, I'm hungry", I said laughing and leaning down to give Sophie a hug, then dapped up with my dude, Paul.

Before I could sit a very, very attractive woman, approached the table.

"Hey Paul, Soph."

"What up Lex", said Paul.

"Hey Lexis" Sophie joined.

" This is my boy Corey. Corey, this is Alexis Parkhurst"

" How are you" I said, trying to hide the immediate impression she made on me?

" Hello."

The way Alexis spoke was similar to starting my Coupe.

Understated and sweet, with just a hint of the power that lay underneath. This woman was thorough from top to bottom. Make-up perfect, lipstick accentuating her full lips, the same as the dress she wore complimented her perfect curves. Ending with the Chanel heels and accessories, including a diamond encrusted Chanel watch.

Either her or her man had a little dough.

I held her chair as she sat down, and then seated myself next to her.

I took in all of her features.
The dreamy light colored eyes, long dark hair, smooth coffee and cream complexion. Her smile alluring and bright, framed by juicy kissable lips. Her face, matched her gorgeous body as well. Toned, hourglass figure that was not too big or too small in any area.
The waiter appeared from nowhere, breaking my concentration and handing out the menus. He poured a glass of champagne for Alexis and one for me.
" Are we ready to order yet or would you like a few minutes?"
" I'm not ready yet", Alexis stated.
" I'll need a minute as well", I said.
"Just let me know, when you're ready."
The waiter smiled and left the table.
At that moment, the host for the evening appeared on stage.
" Ladies and Gentlemen, please help me welcome, Ms. Jessie Alexander."
There was applause throughout the audience, as Jessie took to the stage.

We all watched as the talented singer caressed the microphone and our ears with her sultry voice and smooth, classic jazz.

As we listened to the performance, the waiter returned.

Steak or seafood seemed to be what everyone had on his or her mind for the evening and I pretty much felt like the same.

Within a few moments after everyone had placed their order for dinner, Sophie looked at Alexis a little concerned.

" So how is the fashion show coming, Lex?"

"Horrible!"

" Between dealing with the models and designers, it has been hell to find any rooms for my out of town guest. Apparently my Fashion show is happening the day before the grand opening of that trumped up new nightclub, The Playground."

Paul almost choked on his glass of champagne and Sophie simply looked, wide eyed at what her friend had just said, without realizing.

"All of the hotels close by are booked up."

" So what is trumped up about it, it looks like it is going to be a pretty nice place", I said playing it cool.

" Please! Another teeny, bopper, meat market, hot spot with wet behind the ears girls, serving watered down drinks to ecstasy laced techno heads. Just what the city needs!"

" You can tell all of that by looking at the outside of a building with paper in the windows?"

" Its just the type of establishment that usually opens around here. I've been to them all and no one really innovates anymore. There is nothing new."

" Well…I would like to be the first to let you know that my restaurant and nightclub, will have a little more flavor to it than that and we don't intend to water our drinks down."

Alexis froze for a moment with her mouth open and then laughed, as she realized, that I was the owner of the Playground.

"I am soooo sorry", she giggled, extending her words to emphasize her sincere apology

" I didn't know."

"Uh huh, Insult a man's dream and then laugh in his face when you're caught red handed, I think I'm having my meal delivered", I said feigning indignity.

" Uhm, Lexis, May I re-introduce my friend Corey Woodward, owner of the Playground, nightclub and restaurant that you so aptly dissed…" Paul added.

Sophie just lowered her head trying to conceal her laugh.

" I really am sorry", she said smiling apologetically.

"Yeah, yeah…toying with my emotions. Let's just enjoy our dinner, drinks, music and company…well…"

I left the statement lingering for effect, but smiled.

Now that the ice had been officially broken, we all continued the night, laughing, talking and having a good time.

I found through our conversation that Alexis Parkhurst, was very intelligent, on top of being drop dead gorgeous. A career oriented woman, and a rising star in her field.

A fashion designer, that was preparing to introduce her new line of clothing.

After working for several of the large fashion houses as a coordinator for their shows and studying under some of the top designers around the world, she was preparing to come into her own.

The Alexis Marie, label for couture and A.M.P., her sport line of men, women and children's clothes, had been the entire buzz in the fashion world for months now.

I was looking forward to hopefully attending her show.

"Well, all, I better be getting out of here, I have a long day tomorrow getting my teeny bopper club together."

Alexis, felt comfortable enough to punch my arm.

"Stop", she pouted, " I said I was sorry."

I laughed.

"I'm just kidding", I smiled. " I'm looking forward to your show, I hope you are going to invite me."

"Uh oh, I smell payback", Paul laughed.

"No, no, no, not in the least", I added. " I sincerely am interested in seeing what all of the buzz is about that I have been hearing about this young lady."

" I'll make a deal with you. You invite me to your grand opening and I'll invite you to my fashion show", she said, writing her cell phone number on the back of her business card and handing it to me.

" Let me think about it."

A shocked look crossed her face.

"Just kidding", I laughed.

"Done deal, Miss Parkhurst", I said.

I stood up to leave.

"Check please", Paul called after the waiter

" Paul, you insult me. You know better", I said as I walked towards the door.

"Goodbye all."

The waiter came over to the table and held the chairs for Sophie and then Alexis.
" Mr. Woodward has already taken care of the bill sir", the waiter told them as I exited.
" How did he…" Alexis started.
" Don't even go down that path Lex, we've been trying to figure out how he does that shit forever", Paul laughed.
A few seconds later my car was delivered to the door, I tipped the valet and glanced back as I got in.
"Your friend is shall we say, intriguing", Alexis said as she folded her arms and looked out the window. The moon glistening on the river, and the reflection of my car dancing amongst the waves as I drove off.
"You don't know the half girl", Sophie said.
Paul looked on suspiciously at the two women.
"Can we go now", he said?
"Yes, Love of my life, darling, wonderful man. Getting a little jealous are we", Sophie said kissing him on the cheek?
"Catch you later, Lex."

"Bye lovebirds."

" See you Lex", Paul added.

Paul and Sophie left the bar as Alexis Parkhurst wandered out of the door, towards the promenade, overlooking the river.

There was something about the way Corey Woodward had so easily made her smile. There was something immediate in the attraction. Some sort of electricity in the way he talked and the confidence in which he moved.

For a brief moment she even wondered if he were single and then dismissed the notion from her mind. He's got to have a girlfriend or three hanging around somewhere.

The last man that she had allowed to get close to her actually had two girlfriends and was looking for her to be his third.

Of course the vase, dishes, books and assorted paraphernalia that she threw at him, when she found out, quickly changed his decision.

He fit her type though. Big man. Tall, not all skinny and starving artist type like many of the male models she encountered.

Corey was also a very assured and mature man. A few years older, but that was just fine by her. After all, she liked older men, men with substance and experience.

Alexis pushed the thoughts from her mind and returned to the Valet.

Whatever it was that made this little spark, could wait until a few days from now.

Right now she had a fashion show and launch to think about.

She handed the valet her claim ticket and off he went to retrieve her car. It was only a few moments before he returned with her silver Jaguar and emerged from the vehicle.

Alexis gave him a tip and slid into the driver's seat.

"Thank you ma'am", the valet expressed.

"You're welcome", she said as he closed her car door, and pulled off, headed home to a hot bubble bath and hopefully a relaxing night of sleep.

CHAPTER II

As I began the drive back to my house, I thought about my life until this point.
I could tell there was a little something, something that sparked between Alexis and I, but whether that was going to turn into something or develop into a good friendship or potential business relationship, I didn't know. One thing for sure. I left an impression, as she also had left one with me. Not just the fact that she was drop dead gorgeous, but her personality, her spirit, her intelligence and tenacity as well. I think her stubbornness could probably even rival mine; I thought and chuckled to myself.
She was younger than me, but carried herself in a way beyond her years. Just enough sophistication combined with an earthy and approachable demeanor.

She had that positive entrepreneur vibe, the same, as I would like to imagine I carried as well. My thoughts began to wander. Wander into the paths that led me to where I am today. As positive as the majority of my life was, there was still the aspects of life that no amount of money or connections were going to change. As a matter of fact, money just seemed to complicate the matters even more. I got to where I am, by tenacity, luck and sweat. Starting my career by promoting parties when I was 16 and just kept going. With each party getting, bigger and bigger as I went. Eventually I started doing concerts and events. Bringing in some of the largest stars to perform and later dabbling in real estate. Buying and selling a few houses and also buying 4 apartment buildings. Two in Michigan, 1 in Miami and one in L.A., A salon and spa in New York, where I kept a loft apartment and over the course of 19 years, I amassed 20 million dollars in cash and assets. Not bad for a college dropout from Highland

Park, Michigan. Like most guys from the hood, I went through the ups and downs and the petty jealousies. I went through the robberies and the haters that for some reason didn't want to see me succeed. Even still, there was more darkness. My parents had been in an auto accident, just days after I left college. Leaving my sister and I, to repair the damage in our own relationship as we had stopped talking to each other for a while. Only at the funeral as we laid our parents to rest, did we resolve to work out our differences. I couldn't really remember what it was to throw our relationship into disarray, but just after it happened, the way we treated each other is what kept it going, for almost 3 years.

During that time is when I met Marcy. She was a gorgeous Texas bred, blonde with a body like a black girl. We dated for almost a year and half, before she began to have problems and we wound up breaking up.

My then ex-girlfriend had later been found in an alley, two years ago.

She had developed a co-dependent drug habit of Heroin and crack cocaine.

After our breakup, when the credit card I provided her with, was no longer at her disposal, she took to prostitution as a way to pay for her habits. I never realized the full gamut of what was going on, as she became very adept at hiding things from me when I would see her. Then it got to the point where she just didn't care to hide anything anymore. The dates, the syringe needles, the crack stems. I thought that I would explode when I found out what was going on, but I merely backed away when it became evident that there was nothing that I was going to be able to do. No way to convince her to stop.

I had initially spent months trying to convince her that we could make things work again, if she simply tried. She had access to whatever help she needed, but her pride, her desire to do it on her own, always seemed to jump in the way. Marcy had been hurt by almost everyone in her life.

From her mom passing at an early age, to her dad who abused her, when her stepmother wasn't doing the same thing. Past men in her life, that wanted to treat her as a disposable trophy, her ex-husband who cheated on her. Even her mother-in-law that deceptively sabotaged as much as she could of their marriage. Yes, Marcy had plenty of reasons not to trust anybody. The few people that she could trust, she wound up pushing away. Me included.

I remember it got to the point that the crack heads, prostitutes and drug dealers all knew me by name. Many of my friends were confused as to my journeys into the 7 mile and Charleston area, into the backstreets and crack corridors. Many wondered if I was doing drugs and had developed a habit of my own, or if I was simply toying with the unexpected, the excitement of the street girls that were abundant in that area. Only one guessed that I was there trying to save someone that I dearly cared for. Unfortunately. She didn't want to be saved by me.

My thoughts drifted to the last time we made love.

The drugs had not hidden the fact that she was a very beautiful woman.

Tall and Lanky with dirty blonde colored hair and big beautiful blue eyes.

High cheekbones and a perfect nose. The soft features of her face framed her lips.

She was, in my eyes, Perfect.

Marcy often reminded me of a painting that had come to life, just for me.

I told her that often and she would laugh, blush and tell me to stop it.

The last time I saw her she had come to my house, exhausted as she had been up for days.

Somehow, I seemed to still provide a little bit of comfort for her, despite everything we were going through. At least it seemed that way.

She showered and climbed into bed, cuddled into me and pulled my arm around her waist.

Clutching my hand close to her heart.

I ignored the instant hard-on, the minute her body melted into mine and simply breathed in her scent. Her freshly showered long hair and body, entwined with mine, as we fell asleep.
I was awakened an hour or so later by her kisses on my lips and neck. Her hands pulling insistently at my body. Aroused, I returned the intensity in her passion.
My hands, exploring her body. Tracing down the small of her back, cupping her ass and pulling her leg around my waist. She rolled to her back, pulling me along with her and wrapped both of her long legs around me. Pulling me towards her. I leaned forward. Encircling her nipples with my lips. Flicking the points with my tongue, rapidly and making them stand at attention. I reached for the nightstand. Grabbing the gold foil prophylactic from the drawer. Licking my thumb, I continued to stimulate her body, moving my fingers against her body in slow circles as I ripped the package with my teeth. Her hips began to move closer and harder against my

hand. I moved it momentarily as I rolled the condom down my shaft, and then sank it deep within her, on the first stroke. She was so very, very wet. As I leaned forward to kiss her neck, sucking the tender flesh between my lips, she put her arms around my neck and began pulling me to her body with them and her legs. A few more deep strokes and her back arched. Nails digging into my flesh as she had one orgasm after another.

Her muscles, contracted around my manhood in a powerful spasm

I continued stroking straight through and it got even wilder after that. Pulling, kissing, biting, she slapped my ass and dug her fingers into the muscle. Her legs alternately wrapping around my waist pulling me or rubbing against mine. Her feet brushing over the back of my calves as I continued with everything I had. Sweat forming on my back, until, I finally exploded.

It was like a dam imploding. I realized, it was not just the orgasm, but also all of the stress and tension that had been building up. Suddenly let loose, by our power fuck. It had been forever since the two of us had any sexual dealings and it all ended that night. My body hit the mattress beside her and She positioned herself just under my chin, as her head rested against my chest. Her arms and legs entwined around me as we fell asleep once again. It was the last time that I would see her alive.

Marcy had reached a place in my heart that not many people were ever able to reach. She managed to stir feelings in me that I thought I would never feel again and then as things began to end, she stirred feelings that I never, ever wanted to feel. Like confusion and pain. Like unfulfilled desire and anxiety. It was a veritable cocktail of emotions. Stirred within me and she was either too high or too uncaring to notice what she was doing to me. Too high and irresponsible to realize what she was doing to herself.

Still, she did not deserve to die the way she did. Alone, crumpled like a paper doll in an alley. She had been strangled. The photos that the police showed me, clearly showed the black and blue markings around her neck. The big finger impressions, however did not match mine, as the police may have thought, when they found my business card and a bank stub in her purse from our old account. I explained that we were once a couple before she took to the streets and it seemed to suffice while they investigated further.

I shook the ghost from my mind and my thoughts returned to the present.

Returned to the chance meeting of Alexis with my friends at the restaurant. I couldn't help, but wonder, If Alexis Parkhurst could make me feel as good as Marcy once did …or even as bad as she did, for that matter.

I wondered if there was any reason to be thinking those types of thoughts about Alexis at all.

She's got to have a man or at least a line of them, trying to get at her.

I shook the notion and the daydream from my head as I continued the drive to my house. With that I tapped the accelerator and whisked pass a guy cruising in his mustang GT. Hiding my smirk, I looked over and nodded. Enough of those types of thoughts for one night I told myself. I accelerated even more, feeling the expensive Italian machine growl at the road. Leaving the other cars behind without much of a challenge.

The road, the car and I.

I felt the adrenaline of performance from the vehicle replacing the ghosts and the desires. Replacing temporarily my thoughts of the two women. It was, however, merely a bandage. It was a way to escape for the moment that would return sooner or later.

Trading one form of sensory stimulation for another. The car was almost like another body. Responding to my touch.

We will know soon enough, I thought.

We will know soon enough

CHAPTER III

The view from the terrace of Alexis Parkhurst's riverfront apartment was breathtaking. Sun, water, boats as far as the eye could see. It was pretty easy to see how this setting was inspirational to her creativity. A few days until her fashion show and there were still a million details to attend to. There was a rehearsal later that day and an Interview with a local newspaper, clothes were still being transferred from her shop and From a friends house in Santa Monica and then there was this Corey Woodward thought that kept creeping into her brain. The one that made her want to forget about work and go call him to satisfy her curiosity. This was dangerous though, because to Alexis, being interested in someone meant death. It meant putting thought and effort into something that would most likely not become anything. It meant it could lead to her feelings being enveloped into questions.

It meant taking a chance on the type of scenarios that happened in her last relationship.

Depending on how long it lasted, it could lead to her actually falling in love...and for Alexis Parkhurst that was not a good thing if it was not returned. Not now.

Alexis was the kind of person that loves with her whole heart.

Whereas many of us as humans, fall into interest and have prerequisites and agendas; some rightfully so in this dating game.

When Alexis fell for someone, the only prerequisite was to love her back...with your whole heart.

Mind, body and soul. Sounds like a lot, but at the same time it is nothing. It is a quality that many of us grow out of. As we become adults and realize that not everyone is truthful. Not everyone does things without trying to "get over" on someone.

The simple childlike quality of " I like you" or "I don't like you" is replaced with cynicism, suspicion and emotional baggage from each and every relationship and learning experience that we go through as adults. Yet, here she was. Thinking about the chance meeting last night of one Mr. Corey Woodward. Something about him had sparked an interest and whether it was meant to be a friendship, a business relationship or maybe something a little more, one thing was certain. Alexis, was very interested in him. Tall, with a stocky football player build. Dark chocolate, with soft kissable lips. Just how she liked her men.

There was an air of Intrigue about him as well. The scent of his cologne that somehow she believed that she could still smell. The sense of power and swagger that he had.

" Okay…" Alexis said to herself, but aloud," Enough thinking about this dude" as she shook the thought from her head.

"What Lex", asked Alexis' assistant Katie?

" Just thinking out loud for a second Kate."

Katie had been Alexis Parkhurst's assistant for the past 3 years.
A graduate from Ohio State University in Columbus. 5'3" tall with long black hair. Your not so typical Italian girl. That grew up in the Bronx listening to rap music and dating the star basketball player. Pretty enough to be a model herself. She became friends with Alexis when they both attended college. She was dressed in a Baby Phat cuffed jeans and top, with black studded Giuseppe Zanotti shoes, going over the notes for the fashion show that Alexis had for tomorrow.
" The backdrop is being delivered to the hotel, along with the staging, the DJ is all set with the music and I managed to squeeze three hotel rooms for your guest, other than the suite for yourself."
" That's why I luv ya Kate, you always come through for me ", said Alexis, giving Katie a hug.
"Now…what dude have you had enough thinking about?"

"Why you little asshole", she said laughing, "You heard me in the first place!"

"That's what good assistants are for. Now spill the beans missy. Who, what, when, where and why come?"

" I'm not sure I want to indulge you in my personal gossip, miss", Alexis said laughing.

" ...But Alexis, you know that I live vicariously through your misadventures. You would choose to deprive me of my only enjoyment in life? Deprive me of my own personal, living soap opera? Uh...how selfish can one person be? I tell you." Katie exclaimed.

" Oh my God!! How over the top you are", Alexis said laughing and tossing a pillow after her friend.

"Well, Miss Katie. We will have to indulge you at another time. We have way too much stuff to do. Besides. I just met him and there is no gossip for you. I just thought he had an interesting swag about him. I probably won't ever bump into him again."

"Mmm hmm. Knowing your history, miss sexy. He'll be stalking you within days", Katie said, laughing and walking away with an exaggerated huff.

Alexis simply looked with feigned indignance as her friend walked away.

"Get back to work bitch." said Alexis smiling.

" We need to get over to the hotel and check the set-up for tomorrow's dress rehearsal, then you have a 1 pm late lunch with a reporter from Phathouse magazine."

"I'm ready, let's get out of here."

Alexis grabbed her purse and note pad and the two of them headed out the door for the elevators.

Arriving just as the doors opened for another resident of her floor.

The two stepped into the compartment.

" Phathouse wants to get a few pictures of our before show preparation and then some shots at the actual show. I think today is just going to be the actual interview", said Katie.

" Good. Cause this would not be the day to

photograph all of the chaos we're going through", Alexis said laughing.

"Oh, it hasn't been that bad. You are an old pro at these types of things Lex. Admit it. These things come together for you like a puzzle, now days."

"Its because of I have great assistance from you, missy. I think I would be lost if you hadn't been here. This one is very important for me. It's the introduction of my new line. It's the beginning of…"

Alexis' voice trailed off.

" Lex, It's going to be fine. It's going to be completely beautiful."

" Just a little nervousness."

" Well, why don't you invite your new boyfriend to the show to hold your hand?"

" He actually…" Alexis stopped mid sentence when she realized what she almost said.

" Ooo, I hate you. You know that right?"

" Ha, ha. I knew there was a little more to this story."

Alexis blushed a little.

"Look, I don't exactly know what it is. I just met this dude, but there was something just a little chemical in that first meeting. I'll be straight with you Katie. I'm actually a little confused and embarrassed that I have thought about him, as much as I have already."

" Don't be Lex. That's a good sign…and if he is too stupid to not follow up on it, then it's his loss and you have nothing, I repeat nothing to be embarrassed about."

" You're right. Well, he said he was coming to the show. So we will wait and see."

"You gave him, your number didn't you?"

"I gave him a card, yes…"

"Your personal number, bitch. Don't be playing with me, Ms. Parkhurst ", said Katie, laughing

" Oh, look. First floor!"

The two ladies both laughed and exited the elevator.

" uhm, uhm, uhm", Katie said shaking her head. "What am I going to do with you? You're acting like a blushing little school girl"

"Ok, Stop. Bad enough. I thought about it this much. Let's just get this day over with and try to be prepared for our show in the next couple of days. I repeat, I don't even know, If I will ever see this guy again."

"Alright, miss Parkhurst. I'll cut you some slack. Today only though."

" I feel so lucky."

The two ladies walked over to Alexis' silver Jaguar S-class and with a quick chirp, they were into the car and headed for the Athenaeum, opening the sunroof as her cd player filled the car with her latest musical obsession.

There was assigned parking, but she hadn't wanted to deal with that last night.

As late as it was, she just wanted to hurry into the elevators and up to her sanctuary.

Pulling out of the parking lot, music blasting from the open windows.

Music, fashion, romance, and a fine wine…these were the things Alexis was captivated by.

The things her world had to include to balance out her workaholic ethics…
that, and if there was just not so much traffic on Jefferson avenue today.
Negotiating the lights and tourist staring up at the GM building, sometimes could be like playing a video game. Dodging the “whatever” was thrown at you or exploding around you.
With all of the anxiety that Alexis was feeling, this was not the day that she wanted to deal with anything extra.
A quick dip and one turn around after; they were headed down the street to the hotel.
I guess that wasn’t too bad, Alexis thought to herself, as she pulled into the driveway.
The Valet at the hotel had started to feel like a long lost relative that was in town for a few days, as much as she was seeing him. If she switched radio stations in the car, it would probably throw off his whole day. Alexis laughed to herself at the thought.
The two ladies exited the car and she handed him the keys.

“ Be out in a little while”, she said and turned to follow Katie into the building.

The Valet, and several other men in the vicinity, watched as Alexis glided into the building.

One shaking his head and turning half of his body as he continued a conversation on his cell phone.

When Alexis walked people watched. It was almost like an involuntary response, like that old commercial where a crowd of people would all of a sudden go silent when someone would mention the name of the company.

Her body seemed to float as her hips rhythmically entranced any of the red blooded males in the vicinity. She moved purposefully and gracefully. Knowing the response that she was receiving behind her, but paying no attention to it.

CHAPTER IV

The Playground was going to open in two days and it actually looked like we were ahead of schedule as I met with my general manager, Kenny, to go over the details of our guest performer, YJ. One of the hottest rap artist out right now.

" We have everything from the artist rider and we're all set Corey, we just have to wait on the last of our liquor order and we're set."

" Great Kenny. I have to stop over at the Atheneum to meet with Big Bud from the radio station real quick, and then I'm headed to the crib.

"Alright Corey, I'll finish up here and then check in with you tomorrow."

"Thanks Kenny. Have a good night, my dude."

" Peace."

As I left the club, my cell phone was buzzing.

"Hello", I said into my earpiece.

" What's up playboy? How's the day going so far?"

" Ahead of schedule a little and finally getting closer to some breathing room. Heading over to meet with Big Bud and then home", I said recognizing Paul's voice.

"Cool, cool. So..uh…what did you think of Lex?"

" Dude, we've known each other a very, very long time. You already know what came across my mind, the minute I saw her", I said laughing, " she seems like good people though. Down to earth, with a good sense of humor. She's definitely wifey material from what I saw so far."

" Yeah, she's the total package alright."

" The question of the day, my dude, is does she have a man?"

" Not at present, playboy. Broke up with this playa, playa type dude about a year ago and hasn't really been out with anybody worth mentioning since then."

"Oh yeah?"

"Absolutely. What, you feeling her?"

" Come on man. You know a woman can't look like that and I not have a least a little curiosity."

Oh boy, here we go again, well hit me up tomorrow, man."

"Aight, peace", I replied.

As I reached my car, I noticed a white piece of paper in the wiper blade.

"Motherfu…", I said clenching my teeth and trying to catch myself from getting too upset over the parking ticket, I discovered on my windshield.

Snatching the ticket and hitting the alarm switch on my key fob at the same time, I reminded myself that this was a $140,000 Maserati before I snatched the door off the hinges and got in.

The engine purr, the temperature controlled air starting to blow in the interior of the car, and the custom sound system, I had put in, all springing to life, made me pause. I took a deep breath and released it slowly. There was no reason in the world for me to get upset, over a $10.00 parking ticket, because I didn't get out of the club fast enough to put a couple of coins into the parking meter. Not with a multi-million dollar club opening and driving a Maserati Granturismo, back to a multi-million dollar home in West Bloomfield.

No reason whatsoever…

Pulling onto the street. I adjusted the stereo and headed for the Athenaeum.

My thoughts drifted to Alexis Parkhurst, about 5'7" tall, confident, and sexy.

Lips that I imagined pillowing against mine.

Paul would have to bring her up. I smiled to myself. Blaming Paul for my weak moment.

Maybe, I will give her a call and see how her day is going after my meeting.

Don't want to appear too anxious.

The Athenaeum was just a few short blocks away. The pillars inside of the grand lobby, framed the mythological artwork perfectly. It was like stepping into a small commercial version of Greece. It was commercial, but beautiful.

As I pulled into the parking lot, an attendant approached my car.

" Are you a guest, sir?"

" No, but I am meeting a guest at the bar", I said stepping out of the vehicle and handing him a 10 dollar bill and my keys." I'll probably only be about a half hour."

" Yes, sir", the attendant replied and moved to the side as I stepped away from the car.

I Headed towards the entrance, as the attendant headed towards their board of keys, after slipping a numbered tag onto my windshield.

I had purchased a number of commercials on the radio station and was just meeting up with the program director for a few drinks. A business acquaintance I had known for several years.

He was already at the bar, when I arrived.

"Bud! What's up my dude?" Extending my hand and a hug

"Corey. What it do? Man, I can't wait for that joint of yours to open up. I hear you're going to have naked women dancing in cages", Big Bud said laughing.

" That would be the entertainment in my private office", I replied laughing.

The bartender approached as I sat down.

" How are you tonight sir?"

" Pretty dry, but other than that fairly well. Can I get a Jack and Coke please", I said.

" Coming right up and Another Beer for you sir?"

" Yeah, I'm pretty much done with this one."

" Would you gentlemen like to run a tab?"

" Yeah, that'll work. Thanks."

" So, everything set for the concert? How's tickets been going?"

" We are sold out for opening night. 1000 tickets and Saturday's show is almost sold out as well."

" Sweet. So what time do you need me there to introduce him?"

" I'll send a limo for you about 8pm", I stated.

" Beautiful man…and thanks for the champagne you sent me."

" No problem. They're sponsoring my grand opening…" I said laughing.

" Oh great. Trying to impress the help with your free swag", Bud said.

"Well, you know. We do what we can. Hungry?"

The bartender returned with the drinks.

"Nah. I'm cool. I filled up on pretzels before you got here."

"Ha, ha…so how is the radio business these days?"

" Hectic, hectic, hectic. One promotion after another, but you know…I wouldn't have it any other way, man. You don't seem too excited about your grand opening though."

" You know how that is, my dude. I'm excited about it. It's the first time that I have opened up my own club, where you know, I really am responsible for all aspects.

It's different from just controlling the entertainment schedule. At the same time, its just business, another day on the grind. Trying to make big things happen."

"Well, Playground and your opening concert is definitely big", Bud said.

" Yeah. The only problem now is what do I do for an encore", I said laughing.

I handed an envelope to him, which contained a check for our commercials.

"Thank you", he said.

"No, Thank you", I replied.

" I'm sure you'll think of something my friend. In the meantime, we have about six months of programming that you just provided us with and from what I could see all the shows that you have planned are winners."

" Let's hope so. You know how that kind of thing goes", I said laughing.

" It'll be fine. Don't worry…and we'll pump it up as much as we can at the station."

"I appreciate. A toast, my old friend, to a very profitable year", I said raising my glass.

"To a very profitable year", he said touching his beer to my glass.

Bud took a long draught of his beer and then replaced it on the bar.

"I have to get back to the station Corey. I'll see you in a couple of days my dude."

" Alright Bud. I'll see you then. If you need anything just let me know."

"You too. It's whatever. We got your back."

I stood up and gave him a hug and a handshake.

"Peace", I returned to my seat and took a short sip from my glass and then a long deep breath. In a couple more days, The grand opening of the Playground and another chapter in Detroit's musical history.

As I enjoyed my drink, I looked up to see Alexis Parkhurst walking through the hotel lobby with another young woman carrying a clipboard. Either a secretary or assistant I gathered. She was even more beautiful than I remembered from last night.

Her long hair cascading down her back, past her shoulders.

She was wearing heels and a pair of jeans that looked painted onto her lower body.

Her and her girl stopped at the main counter and I decided to make my presence known.

I let the bartender know that I was headed over to the reservations desk for a moment and motioned towards the two women.

Walking over to where they were standing, I took in every detail of Alexis' taught frame.

She was still pre-occupied at the counter when I reached them.

" You know there are some serious laws that can come into play, with the way you are stalking me", I said approaching the two women.

She turned and immediately began smiling.

" Well Mr. Woodward, I suppose I will just have to convince you, not to turn me in."

I smiled. Even though I believe I was already smiling at the sight of her.

" So how are you today?"

" A nervous wreck, but other than that I'm doing ok and you?"

" Finally unwinding from being a nervous wreck all week", I said laughing.

" Corey, this is my assistant Katie. Katie, Corey Woodward, the owner of the Playground. The restaurant and nightclub opening up this Friday."

" Hello."

" Hey, How are you?"

" Congratulations on your club opening. Looks like it's going to be a pretty hot spot."

"Thank you. Hopefully you're right ", I said laughing.

" So, are you spying on my show", Alexis added playfully.

"Actually, I just met with one of the radio station people in the bar. Is this where your show is going to be held", acting as if I didn't know.

"Yes, it is Mr. Woodward", she said. " You forgot already?"

" I had a really late night last night. Too much Champagne", I joked.

" We're just heading over to check some last minute details."

"Hmmm, working…what a shame. I was just going to invite you two to share a drink with me."

" Why don't you go ahead Lex? I'll run up and make sure the backdrop and everything is in place", said Katie.

" Well…uh…perhaps one. Kate, I'll be up in a moment."

" Nice to meet you Mr. Woodward. I look forward to coming to your club after the opening", said Katie extending her hand.

" Actually Corey invited me to the opening, I was going to drag you with me anyway", Alexis added laughing as I shook Katie's hand.

" Wow. What a great boss", Katie added sarcastically. " Are you coming to the fashion show tomorrow, Mr. Woodward?"

" Corey… And I wouldn't miss it for the world", I said.

" Ok. Well I will see you there. See you in a minute Alexis."

" Ok."

Katie headed for the elevators as Alexis and I headed for the bar. Once there I held the stool as she glided into it.

" Your pleasure for the day, Madame", I asked as the bartender arrived.

" I hear that this establishment makes an absolutely sinful chocolate martini."

" Then a chocolate Martini is what we shall have. Bartender. A chocolate martini for the lady and another Jack and Coke for me."

" Coming right up sir."

" So, Ms Parkhurst, what made you decide to venture into your own line?"

" Its just something I have always wanted to do. I've worked with so many great designers, it was really just a matter of wanting to add my own voice to the mix."

" Do you already know what stores are going to carry it?"

" Not as of yet. There are a few more shows and I have a sales representative from

Chicago, one from New York and one from L.A., that will all be attending this show. So. Somewhere after that, they will let me know what stores are interested."

" Sounds like you have everything well in hand. Congratulations."

Our drinks arrived and I proposed a toast to our new ventures. We talked and laughed casually as we sipped our drinks. Getting to know a little more about each other. Getting personal.

" You know Corey…If I didn't know better, I would swear that you were trying to get to know me for some personal reason"; Alexis said sipping the last of her drink.

" Well…maybe I am a little guilty of that. It's the perfume you are wearing, I swear.

It does something to just render me helpless. What are you wearing?"

"Its called Obsess" She shared. "Its one of my favorite fragrances."

"See. That makes sense. Soft, seductive, beautiful…just like you…and its definitely working"

" You know, you can't keep saying things like that. I'm going to think you're trying to more than get to know me."

" Then, I suppose if I ask you out tonight after work, that you will know for sure", I said looking directly into her eyes.

Alexis looked a little surprised, but not disappointed.

" I suppose that I would…and where would you like to take me?"

"It's a surprise. Say, I pick you up at about 10?"

" Ok. Call me…and I will see you tonight. In the meantime, I better get upstairs and act like I am actually working today."

"I will see you tonight", I said standing up.

"So, what should I wear tonight for this surprise?"

" Casual. No heels", I said.

" I'll see you later."

" Until then", I said.

Alexis turned and walked out of the bar into the lobby. She was almost to the elevators before she looked back with a smile on her face. She knew that I would be watching, even though I was trying to be nonchalant about it. The little mischievous smirk on her face said it all. It said, "Yeah, I know you want it." ...and she was correct about that.

As I watched her from the corner of my eye, I wondered, if that was what she was really thinking at that particular moment.

They say patience is a virtue and I suppose at long last in my life, I was starting to understand that statement.

I finished my drink, paid the tab and headed for the front door. I was looking forward to whatever the night would bring.

I handed the valet my ticket stub and he returned with my keys.

I had a nice little drive ahead of me from downtown Detroit to Bloomfield, but it was a beautiful day. Not too hot and just perfect for cruising.

I let all of the windows down and pulled out of the driveway into the Greek town traffic.

A few quick turns and I would be on the highway, fortunately enough past rush hour that my drive would be uninterrupted or at least, uninterrupted by traffic.

I adjusted the stereo and leaned back into the head cushion. My thoughts switched to Alexis. There was the tingle of anticipation cursing its way through my body. I still had not felt that type of anticipation about my club, as of yet.

I breathed in deeply and exhaled in one motion.

Then gunned the big engine and gave in to the thrill of my ride. Thus postponing my thoughts and my anticipation of Alexis Parkhurst.

I would see her soon enough and perhaps some of my curiosity would be satisfied.

CHAPTER V

The phone rang twice before Alexis answered it. Her sultry and seductive voice cooing through the receiver.

"Hello."

" Hey, Lexis. Corey."

" Well, Hello sir. On your way", she asked?

" Yes, I have one problem though. I don't know where you live."

"That might make things a little difficult."

" Just a little bit."

"I live at Riverview", she stated. " Just pull up to the guard shack and give them my name. They will call up."

" Alright. I should be there in about 10 minutes."

" I'll be here. You're still not going to tell me where we are going?"

" mmm, Not yet. Maybe when I pick you up. Or maybe I will just torture you until the last minute."

"Losing points Mr. Woodward. I'm not into S&M."

" I'll see you in a minute", I said smiling.

We both hung up and I eased back into the plush seats of my Chrysler 300C limousine. Lowering the privacy window, I informed Barry, my driver of our destination.

"Riverfront Apartments, Barry."

"Yes sir", He responded

I closed the privacy partition again and turned up the stereo.

Riverview Apartments and Condominiums are 4 towers, gleaming behemoth like on the Detroit River. Complete with boat docks, its own grocery store, dry cleaners, health club, etc., etc. with some of their condos in the half million dollar range.

A few brief moments later, we were pulling into the driveway at the apartment complex. As we approached the guard shack, I lowered my window.

" Good evening. May I help you", the guard asked?

" Alexis Parkhurst", I replied.

" …And you are?"

" Corey Woodward."

" Just a moment, Sir."

The guard returned to his booth and dialed Alexis' apartment.

" Miss Parkhurst, there is a Corey Woodward to see you."

After listening for a moment, he replied with a Yes, ma'am and returned the receiver to The base.

"If you pull over to the east entrance, she will be right down sir."

"Thank you", I replied and closed the window as Barry put the car in motion.

We pulled over to the entrance and a few moments later, Alexis emerged from the towers.

I stepped out so Alexis would know which vehicle.

" Hmmm, Limousine Mr. Woodward?"

" Yeah, I figured if you got me drunk and tried to take advantage of me, I had better have someone to drive me home", I joked.

“ You are silly”, she laughed and got into the car, after giving me a quick hug.

I followed into the rear compartment and Barry, closed the door.

Barry pulled the big Chrysler around the curve and out of the parking area.

“ Champagne”, I asked?

“Yes, Please…”

Alexis was dressed in form fitting button down type blouse with Capri style pants and flats, as I had informed her no heels. I could see a jeweled belly chain sneak a peek from the bottom of her blouse that showed just a hint of her tight stomach. Diamond earrings, bracelet and watch completed her look. Casual, upscale and sexy. Even though I believe this woman could wear a burlap sack and look sexy.

I poured a glass of champagne for her and one for myself.

“So is it still a surprise, where you are taking me?”

“ A friend of mine is DJ’ ing a rave tonight.”

"A what", she laughed. "You're taking me to a rave?"

"Not into that" I asked?

" Its, not that. You are just slightly surprising."

" Surprising?"

" Well, the few people that get up the nerve to ask me out, definitely don't figure I would be comfortable at something like that and mistakenly, I didn't picture you as a person that would go to something like that. Very cool, Mr. Woodward. Very cool", she said tapping her glass against mine and taking a sip of her champagne.

" Well…it's a little more upscale and commercial than your standard rave. Besides, You don't scare me", I laughed. " Did you have a chance to relax a little?"

" Oh my God! This has been the first time that I have actually had a chance to take a short break, since deciding to launch my line."

" I know what you mean. I have been running around like crazy, trying to get Playground open."

" Perfect timing for a rescue, Corey."

" Thank you…and believe me, I appreciate you rescuing me." I smiled. " I needed to get away at least for a little while and not stress over details."

" To a stress free night", she said proposing a toast.

" To a stress free night", I returned and saluted with my glass.

" Are these c.d.'s", She asked. Gesturing towards a case on the opposite seat.

" Yeah, you want to listen to something?"

" I want to check out your musical taste", she said with a mischievous look on her face.

" Feel free", I said handing her the black case that held some of my compact disc.

Opening the case, she immediately found something that she liked.

" Ooh, can we listen to this", she said clutching the c.d. like a prize. "I've been meaning to get out to buy this."

" Whatever you'd like", I said taking the c.d. and placing it into the limousine's player.

" You have a pretty nice variety. We might actually be able to get along", she laughed.
" Music is pretty important to a concert promoter", I said.
" Oh. That's right. I almost forgot what you do other than the club."
" They say the mind is the first thing to go", I joked.
" Ah...Meany", she said playfully punching my arm.
Time seemed to stand still as the limo cruised up I-75 towards Ferndale and there never seemed a lapse in conversation. It was if I had known Alexis all of my life. Yet we were just really getting to know each other.
Likes, dislikes, Careers, plans for the future. Almost too quickly the conversation was about to be put on hold as the limo pulled onto 9 mile off the freeway.
Fortunately at this time of night, there was very little traffic and we soon found ourselves in front of The Magic lounge on Woodward Avenue.

There was a crowded line at the front entrance as we emerged from the limo and headed straight for the door, directly to the portable human mountain that was guarding the entrance.

" Corey Woodward plus one", I said as I approached the security guard.

" Guest list", the man said into the microphone attachment hanging from his ear.

"Cory Woodward."

" Confirmed plus one", crackled the response back through the receiver.

Lifting the hook on the velvet crowd control, he ushered us into the club's entrance.

We were immediately swept into another world as lights, fog and music engulfed our senses.

This was dance culture. Detroit style and everyone was representing. The room swirled from strobe lights to pitch black. Illuminated at times only by the iridescent shine of a hundred glow lights.

Alexis and I kind of drifted into the middle of the crowd. Moved by the rhythm of the room. My DJ friend, Jenna, held the audience captive with the beat heavy selections she chose. For the next 3 hours, we danced, and watched as the various guest dee jay's, all added their own vibe to the night.

I finally got the opportunity to introduce Alexis to Jenna and let her know that I had made it out to support her and with that accomplished it was time to get out of there. This party was probably going to go until 6am and I just couldn't afford that luxury this week.

With all of the goodbyes and the pleasantries out of the way, Alexis and I made our way out of the building and back to the limo.

" Hungry", I asked.

" I could eat ", she replied.

" Good. I know the perfect place", I said pouring two glasses of champagne.

Alexis looked at me with those dazzling eyes. It was as if she had really just taken a good look at me.

"I bet you do, Mr. Woodward", she finally replied, taking a sip from her glass.

" Barry, we're going to stop and get something to eat", I said through the intercom to my driver.

" Yes, sir, He replied.

I was beginning to like the playful banter between Alexis and I. She was flirty and laid back and to top it off had an easy manner and infectious smile.

As I stared into her eyes, I wondered what she was thinking to herself at that moment.

If I was having the same effect on her, as she was having on me. It was plain that she was interested, but how far were we going to take this.

I decided that I was just going to ride it out. Whatever happens happens.

After my experience with Marcy, I found myself to be cautious and deeply reflective about my past experiences and the relationships that presented themselves to me. So much so that I found myself not taking the opportunities that were presented to me at times. This was not going to be one of those times.

Now with the club about to open, it had made me seem even more reclusive.

It was work, club, home, rinse and repeat, though I was more than ready to break out of my self-imposed hibernation.

There was also the baggage of mistrust. Especially, when just meeting someone, and most definitely meeting someone as beautiful as Alexis.

There is always the question of who else is she seeing, Is there anyone close to getting serious with them. I hate competition. Even for someone like me with the assets I have, it is still a game of chance and swimming with sharks in this dating pool and if I like someone it was guaranteed there were a bunch of people that felt the same way.

Of course if there were not some sort of slightly strong interest, it wouldn't even matter.

Its those times that you actually want to explore things to the fullest, that all of these thoughts come into play and it was a little awkward, to say the least.

Now, with the very attractive, smiling and laughing, Alexis, sitting across from me in the Back of my limo, it was hard to not, think these thoughts.

" So what type of food do you like", I asked?

" I'm flexible. Pretty much anything" , she said.

" Well there is Italian, French, Coney, pizza, falafels, vegetarian all right in this area."

We mutually decided on an Italian restaurant, situated on the corner of the block.

Barry wheeled the car around the corner and pulled into the parking lot in back.

My brain was already making my taste buds believe I could taste the pasta and Parmesan.

Barry removed himself from the front driver compartment and opened the rear door for us to exit.

Alexis stepped out of the vehicle first and I followed close behind. There were minimal stares as we exited and walked briskly into the restaurant.

Basically people wondering if they had seen us before. As if some new celebrity was sneaking into the restaurant attempting to be discrete.

We entered and caught the attention of the Maitre D.

Ordering a table for two, Alexis and I, waited patiently for a table and then followed him as he led us through a labyrinth of tables and chairs.

Once seated, the waiter came over and gave each of us a menu.

" Would you like to start with something from the bar", asked the waiter.

" Alexis?"

" Just a water please."

" I'll have a water as well." I said to the waiter. " Probably wouldn't be too wise to mix Champagne with other alcohols."

" Coming right up" he said.

The waiter left to get our drinks as we got comfortable at our table.

Scanning the menu quickly, I decided on the Veal Parmesan, Spaghetti and Garlic bread.

Alexis chose the shrimp scampi and we waited for the waiter to return to place our order.

It wasn't long after placing our menus on the table that he returned and took our food order.

It was only a few minutes after that, he returned with our drinks.

Alexis took a deep breath, enjoying the flavor in the air of the restaurant.

Our senses stimulated by the aroma and the ambiance.

She then focused on me. Her eyes sparkling as she looked deep within mine.

" So are you having a good time", I asked her?

" Mm, hmm. Definitely."

" I meant to tell you this earlier, but, I find you to be extremely beautiful and captivating", I said.

Alexis looked pleasantly surprised, smiled and blushed.

"Planning out what you want to say to me?"

"No, nothing like that. I just meant to say it a while ago when we were in the limo, but we were talking and laughing and it just didn't come out."

" Well, I'm not sure what to say to that, other than Thank you."

" Even that is more than necessary. Its simply the truth."

She hesitated a moment. Staring down into her water glass, her thumbs playing along the rim.

" I think I don't know what to say, because a part of me, was hoping that you found me attractive and another part of me was afraid that you would."

" That is a very confusing statement, Miss Parkhurst", I said.

" Yes. I suppose that it is", she smiled. " Let's just say that I have had more than my share of bad relationships and players in my life."

" I see", I replied. "So you think I'm a player?"

" Too early to tell, but let's also say that there is something about you, that I haven't been able to put my finger on yet. Its as if we were destined to meet. I think that we are definitely going to become the best of friends Mr. Woodward or…"

Her voice trailed off momentarily.

" Or something else entirely", she finished.

" You are definitely not alone on the bad relationship experiences. I have really had more than my share."

She looked at me and smiled.

" Then we shall see what we shall see", she said.

" That we will. It has been said that everyone enters your life for a reason, a season or a lifetime, we just have to see which one it is", I smiled.

I looked deep within the hazel pools that Alexis used to view the world.

I couldn't help it. I was hypnotized.

Fortunately for me the waiter reappeared with the dinner salads that came with our meal. We both smiled and separated as he placed the dishes on the table. An assortment of salad dressings and he was away.

Our meal continued, laughing and talking throughout. Alexis made me feel very comfortable. It was almost if we had known each other since childhood.

I really couldn't explain it. I had never connected with someone so easily…or so quickly for that matter.

After dinner, I grabbed a couple of mints at the door as we went back to the limousine.

Alexis noticed as I was opening the small packet.

" What do you need that for", she asked, once again with her mischievous look?

I paused. Looking at her as she took the mint from my hand and popped it into her mouth.

I smiled, as she turned and headed out of the door. I opened the other mint and placed it in my mouth.

Barry was parked just out of the back door.

" I suppose, I should get you home. You have a very big day tomorrow."

" I have a very big day…today", she corrected!

" I suppose you are right", I laughed.

As we got into the vehicle, I slid close to her. Barry pulled the car onto 9 mile and Alexis leaned against me. Her back to my chest and her arms folded.

" You don't mind do you", she asked?

" Not at all", I replied.

I slid an arm around her and she adjusted even more. She turned slightly to look at me and as she did there was a question in her eyes.

That question was answered when I closed the small distance between us. Hoping that this was the answer she sought.

Our lips touched. Then touched again more passionately. Her hand came around and rested upon my cheek. Gently pulling me closer to her kisses.

I reached for her waist, resting my hand just above her hip and continued to explore her lips and tongue with my own. She returned my kisses. Her tongue, dancing with mine.

Damn this woman could kiss.

As we parted, coming up for air, she laid her head against my chest.

Fortunately, words were unnecessary at this point, because for the life of me, I couldn't think of any.

I rested my head against the leather of the seat. Closing my eyes as we rode down I-75, towards her apartment.

She took a deep breath and snuggled closer to me.

Where this night was going to take things in the future, I didn't know.

However, I was prepared to follow.

The short ride back to her apartment continued in silence, except for the soft and occasional sighs as we cuddled.

When we arrived and Barry opened the door, I followed her to the entrance of the building.

“ So you will be at my show tonight?”

“ Wouldn’t miss it for the world”, I replied.

“ You better not. I will see you tonight then, Mr. Woodward”, she said.

“ Tonight”, I repeated and gave her a kiss goodnight.

“ Good night Corey”, she said. Turning to enter the building.

I returned to the limousine. As I settled into the rear compartment of the car, I took a deep breath. We had just crossed one of the very critical unsure lines.

That moment where it is obvious that two people are interested in each other.

Where you may want to see them, but it is not definite whether you will or you won’t or what will happen or what the best thing to do is.

It was this type of dynamic, between a man and a woman where logic and feelings are temporarily out of sync, that anything could happen…and usually did.

Its where, logically you tell your brain that you just met and you do the things that you are supposed to do like go to work, clean your house. The daily things that you go through the motions on, but your feelings are running their own agenda. Where little thoughts of the person keep popping up and you find yourself simply wanting to talk to or be with that person.

However, you don't want to impose, you don't want to bug them or seem needy or like a stalker…and above all else…Not to look like a fool.

Should you invest time and actual effort into seeing what could happen or do you simply sit back and not do anything, waiting to see what happens. That is the big question. …

and that type of question only happens, when you actually like someone.

I decided that the best thing for me to do is to wait and see. After all, there was no indication that I should do anything else, even if I could.

I adjusted the stereo and eased my head back. The wonderful perk of having a driver.

I could go ahead and nap on my way home. I closed my eyes, enjoying the smooth hum of the engine, the music pulsating against the rhythm of the road.

The next thing I knew, we were pulling into the driveway of my home. I had fallen into a relaxing power nap as we drove. Tomorrow, I had to make some last minute checks on the club and then later I would check out Alexis' fashion show.

I bid a goodnight to Barry as I traveled up the walkway to my house. Barry waited until I had opened the door and was inside, before pulling the big vehicle around to the back, near his loft on the property.

Tonight was a very good first date, I thought, as I walked up the stairs.

Even as exhausted as I was, a smile formed on my face. It had been meetings all day, dancing all night and that kiss from Alexis. It was a good exhaustion.

The kind of exhaustion I didn't mind if it meant money and a woman like Alexis.

CHAPTER VI

Morning came with little fanfare. Correction. The fanfare this particular morning came with was my cell phone going off at 8am.

" What it do Pimpin", Paul asked as I groggily answered the phone.

" What up doh", I replied.

" Where were you hiding last night?"

" I went to Jenna's thing at the Magic."

"Oh yeah? I forgot about that. How was it?"

I paused momentarily.

" With Alexis Parkhurst…"

" What?!"

" You heard me. Alexis and I, went to Jenna's party last night", I said ignoring his other questions.

" How did that shit happen?"

" Remember I went to see Big bud over at the Athenaeum."

" Yeah, that's where Lex has her fashion show happening…ohhhh, you ran into her over there."

" Yep, yep. We had a couple of drinks and I invited her to go out with me that night."

" So what happened?"

" We went to the club, we danced, we drank champagne, and I dropped her off at home."

" You must think I was born yesterday night. What else happened?"

" That's pretty much about it", I said.

" Corey! Mr. Champagne in the limousine, people running around to do your bidding, VIP into the club, lying ass…nothing happened?"

"Alright, alright already. We kissed", I admitted.

" Kissed?"

" We kissed."

"That's it", Paul said inquisitively.

" Dude, Yes. What do you expect? It's the first time we went out."

" Let's just say that I saw the look she gave you when you left the restaurant the other night. She looked like she wanted to cover you in whip cream and dip chocolate chip cookies in you."

" For real?"

" For real, for real."

" So what's up?"

" Well you know her fashion show is tonight."

" Yeah. You and Sophie are still going right?"

" Yeah, we're going."

" Why don't I have Barry pick you guys up and we all go together?"

" Bet. We'll be ready about 7:30."

" Alright man. See you guys tonight."

" Cool. Hey uh…Corey."

" Yeah."

" Alexis is a big girl true enough, but uh…take it easy on her okay."

" You know I'm not like that my dude. I'm not hard on women at all"

" Yeah. I know. It's just that Alexis is one of a kind. She's had almost as many bad breaks as you, my dude. Hopefully you two have a good time… at whatever happens out of this."

" Its cool. I really liked just hanging with her. She's good people."

" Alright. I'll see you tonight."

" Peace", I said " Hanging up the phone."

I rolled over and stretched out on the bed. The sun was beaming through my window.

I fiddled for the stereo remote and hit the power button upon retrieving it.

As the music escaped the speakers, I pulled myself from beneath the sheets and comforter and headed for the bathroom.

I had a shower with 10 massage heads and I turned on every one of them. As soon as the water was the right temperature I slipped in. Letting the jets ease away all the tension and relax me. I stood there for a moment with my eyes closed, just enjoying the sensations as the water hit my body. Thinking about Alexis.

I couldn't help, but wonder, if the rest of her tasted as good as those juicy lips I sampled last night.

Kissing Alexis simply made me hungry for more. The way her soft body molded into my hands and she pressed hungrily against me. Shaking the thought and beads of water from my head, I continued my shower.

Today was going to be an interesting day, to say the least. I couldn't wait for her fashion show and to see her designs. Okay, I thought, I couldn't wait for her fashion show to see, HER. I admitted to myself.

As I finished my shower and stepped out, grabbing at the thick terry cloth towels on the stand next to it, I thought about the dreaded today, to do list. I realized. There wasn't much for me to handle. The artist performing at the club would arrive tonight. Barry would pick them up at the airport. The hotel was already taken care of. The club was stocked. I just needed to run by and do a last minute check on things. The show was sold out, so I didn't need to call the ticketing company. Okay, maybe today was going to be not that bad after all. I finished toweling off. I had a little time to kill, so this was going to be a good breakfast day and some relax time in front of the plasma screen before I needed to get dressed and out the door. This was going to be an Armani from head to toe day as well. From the cologne to the socks, I thought.

Walking into my closet, off the bedroom, I pulled the suit off the rack and stepped back in towards my bed. Might as well go all the way and do the diamonds today as well.

I laid the clothing items on my bed, black Armani boxers, black socks, grey shirt with black tie. I threw on the boxers and grabbed my robe. Venturing down to the kitchen.

" Good morning, Mr. Woodward", Louisa said as I walked in.

Louisa was my housekeeper and cook. She was going over a grocery list when I walked in.

" Would you like breakfast today?"

She was used to me grabbing a bagel and juice and running out the door. Mind racing with details of this, that and all the other things I had to accomplish.

"Actually, Yes, Louisa. How are you today?"

" I'm doing good, Mr. Woodward. What would you like for breakfast?"

" Omelet, juice, toast, potatoes", I said already tasting the food.

Louisa was an excellent cook and she knew exactly how I liked my Omelet. Three types of cheese, onions, green and red peppers, crumbled sausage and my potatoes seasoned. There was nothing like a big breakfast to start the day, Except, of course, being awakened by a gorgeous woman in your bed, breakfast and then back to bed for the rest of the day.

I would have to say that, that one would top my best of list.

It had been a while, since I had enjoyed that type of day. I had too many things to accomplish all the time. I grabbed the mail from the counter where Louisa had placed it and returned to the kitchen table, beginning the process of opening and reading the accumulated mail at my house. Easing back into my chair and making myself comfortable as I waited on breakfast. In mere moments the enticing smell of the food cooking filled the downstairs area as Louisa prepared what I requested.

When she finished preparing the potatoes and the omelet she brought it to the table.

"Juice?"

" Yes Please. Papaya", I said.

Luisa moved over to the refrigerator removing the juice and stepping over to one of the kitchen cabinets. Retrieving a glass, she turned to the refrigerator door, pushing on the handle and getting crushed ice from the icemaker. After pouring me a glass and delivering it to the table.

I'm heading to the market now Mr. Woodward, Is there anything new or special you need?"

" No. I think we're fine Louisa. Have Barry take you. I should be ready by the time that you guys get back."

"Alright, Mr. Woodward. See you in a little while."

I said a silent prayer, blessing my food before partaking. I was looking forward to today. Even with my club opening tomorrow, my interest was distracted.

Alexis had wet my appetite, last night. I wanted more.

CHAPTER VII

The Alarm clock sounded like a parade passing through the hallway of the apartment building when it buzzed Alexis awake. Katie had already let herself into the apartment and was hard at work when she heard the ringing from Alexis' room. After a few moments she knocked on the door and then slowly entered.

" Lex? Time to make the donuts, girl", she joked.

" Ugh…Too much Champagne", she mumbled.

" I guess that and your present hangover could be interpreted as a good thing?"

"Avoid hangovers, Stay drunk", Alexis grumbled, pulling a pillow over her head!

" Alright, missy. Suck it up. This definitely is not the day, that you can afford the luxury of staying in bed."

" Mornings are evil", Alexis whined from beneath the pillow!
" I take it your outing last night was good", Katie said laughing.
Alexis turned over and tossed the pillow from her head to the side.
" That man has kisses that make you believe in God", She said breathing out loudly!
" Wohhh!! What???!!! Did I miss something here? What happened? Did you guys hook up?"
" No, Thank God! I'm afraid to have sex with him now. I don't want to take the chance of spoiling the fantasy."
Katie laughed loudly and high fived Alexis, who joined in hearing her friend laughing and realizing what she had just said.
" Okay. Kisses were that good huh?"
" We just had a really good time. Went to a dance club, where a friend of his was deejaying and then out to eat at this little Italian place. Then he brought me home and

somewhere in the middle of all of this, we kissed."

" Oh my", Katie said.

" I forgot to mention that all of this hanging out was done while sipping champagne in his limousine."

" He rented a limo for you guys?"

"No. He "Owns" a limo."

" Ah ha! That's the problem right there. Too much Champagne", both women laughed.

" Didn't I just say that", Alexis laughed.

" Sounds like you had a really good time. I'm happy for you. I was starting to worry about you, after Lewis."

" Lewis is old news. Ancient Black History if that is what you are referring to" Alexis offered.

" Well, you know, it has been a while."

" I have been on dates, since Lew", Alexis said sitting straight up in the bed.

" True. Yes, but not one like this, someone that is in your league.

Some of those guys you went out with, weren't even in the vicinity of your league, by blocks and cities", Katie laughed at the analogy.

"Whatever, missy. I'm getting in the shower. Let's get this day cracking."

" As soon as you're ready Lex, we can jet over to the hotel and double check everyone's rotation and get ready for the run through. I talked with a couple of the stores that were selling tickets. It should be a packed house tonight."

"That's always a good thing"; Alexis said walking across the room.

" At $30.00 a ticket, that's a very good thing", Katie laughed.

Alexis simply smiled and walked into the bathroom. Turning on the shower and cranking up the music on her bathroom radio.

The brief little episode last night crossed her mind and she wondered what the night would bring as she stepped into the shower stall. The hydrotherapy, massage jets relieving the tension in her body as they pulsed the hot water onto her

Alexis closed her eyes and absentmindedly ran her hands along her body, enjoying the shower. The excitement of her show was turning into butterflies in her stomach or was it the memory of Corey's lips brushing softly against her own, then pressing insistent and urgent against her mouth.

She took a deep breath and reached for the bath beads and loufa.

Her mind began to wonder, as did her hands. The combination of the hot water pulsing against her body and thoughts of Corey was affecting her erotically. Before she realized what she was doing, she had begun to touch herself, very intimately.

"If only you knew Corey Woodward…if only you knew", she thought, before continuing her shower and foregoing the intimate self-exploration.

CHAPTER VIII

The rest of the day went by pretty quickly and before we knew it, the time for the fashion show was upon us. I arrived to pick up Sophie and Paul at 7:30 on the nose and we rushed down I-75 to get to the hotel on time Fortunately there was no traffic heading downtown at that time. We arrived at the Athenaeum hotel at 8:15pm, with the show starting at 8:30 pm. There was still a large crowd slowly making its way up the elevators to the ballroom where the show was to be held. Alexis was somewhere backstage, double and triple checking that everything went as planned, and what a plan it was. Sophie hightailed to the stage area, as the show was to begin with a musical performance from her. The band was already on stage and ready to go. She joined them. Whispering hellos and offering hugs to her friends and then went over to the microphone. A woman appeared onstage and walked over to another microphone. She was wearing a black Alexis Marie T-shirt and black slacks with heels.

“ Ladies and Gentlemen. Welcome to the first Alexis Marie Parkhurst and Friends Benefit and Fashion show. We have an extraordinary evening planned for you and we sincerely hope that you enjoy. As you all know, a portion of the proceeds from your ticket purchase will be going to several of our favorite charities. There is information on them all at the front table, near the door you entered through. We sincerely hope you allow some time to learn about them and support them. Now, without further ado, we would like to start the evening with the very beautiful, very talented, Miss Sophia Deschanel.”

The audience applauded as the drummer gave a four count and the band sprang to life.

Sophie commanded the stage and ran through her material with her brand new group, segueing into a skit from one of the guest designers. The elaborate production was amazing. Sophie's musical set was augmented with a live deejay that took over the musical accompaniment of the show as the designers and models presented their craft. Lights and fog were activated as the show progressed. It was like being at a rock concert that somehow turned into a fashion show.

Each designers segment had their time slot and specific models. As the evening wound down it was time for the Alexis Marie segment. As the lights dimmed some hip-hop, and rock music drifted from the speakers as fog began to well up on the stage.

Suggestive lighting enveloped the models as they took their positions on the stage. Two huge signs proclaiming Alexis Marie were revealed when the lighting changed. The signs were previously wrapped behind huge black curtains and were pulled away as the show began. The designs Alexis created were stunning.

Her eveningwear consisted of several hand-beaded pieces that must have taken months to complete, I thought. At the end of the show, Alexis appeared on the runway. She was wearing a black dress, suggestively hugging her curves. A diamond chain that hung down like a rapper, that said AMP and calf length Roberto Cavalli boots.

A bright, proud smile graced her beautiful face. I could see an expression of relief as the crowd stood and gave her a standing ovation. She spotted me in the front row of the audience and gave me a wink before taking a bow and exiting the stage, the applause still ringing after she had left.

Sophie looked over at me.

" Should I even ask, what "THAT" was all about" she smiled?

" No. You should not", I replied.

Paul just looked up towards the ceiling and pretended to be whistling.

I laughed as Sophie looked at both us, knowing something was up.

Paul, Sophie and I, all got up and went towards the side stage area and waited for

Alexis. She emerged moments later and began shaking hands with her well wishers and came over to where we were standing.

Sophie hugged her tightly.

"I'm so proud of you girl", she exclaimed.

She hugged Paul and then turned to me.

Smiling sort of shyly.

" If you don't get over here and give me a hug…" I said mock menacingly.

Alexis smiled and complied with my hug request. She was beaming and fidgety.

Glowing with her success.

Katie came from behind stage and over to where we were all standing.

The clothes were all being packed away, so they could go back to Alexis's shop and the crew for the staging would arrive in the morning to take everything down. There were three cameramen that documented the show on video and I'm sure these things would wind up on You Tube or something any day now.

" You pulled it off again, Miss Alexis", Katie said smiling.

" We pulled it off", Alexis corrected her, giving her a huge bear hug.

" I'm going to make sure everything gets back to the warehouse and then I will see you in the morning Lex."

" Alright you. Don't get into too much trouble tonight. Save that for tomorrow", Alexis said laughing.

Katie looked at her with a sarcastic smirk.

" Mmm hmm. You too", she said leaving with a smile

With the show over, Paul, Sophie, Alexis and I, piled back into my limousine.

Paul and Sophie were anxious to return to their home in Troy, while Alexis and I opted to stop and grab some food. After we dropped them off I suggested a Japanese restaurant nearby, since it was relatively close and Alexis agreed that Asian food was sounding really good about now. The restaurant was located in an upscale mall complex a few short miles away from where Paul and Sophie lived. I called the restaurant manager, a friend of mine and after exchanging a few pleasantries; he had to handle some business in the restaurant. He gave the phone to one of his waitresses to take our order. Asking her to take care of his friends. We ordered. Chicken for me and Fish for Alexis, along with Rice and vegetables. All the things a growing body needs. Alexis moved closer to me as we drove to the restaurant.

" That was a great show today Lex. I really enjoyed myself", I said.

" You enjoyed all of the hot women strutting in front of you. You're not fooling me Corey Woodward", she said.

" I'm crushed. How could you think such a thing about me", I asked?

" Sure you are", she said, folding her arms.

" Do I detect a little possessiveness creeping out?"

"No", Alexis said, way to fast for it to not be funny. Like a little girl caught with her hand in the cookie jar. I smiled.

“ Now why would I stare at them, when I get to eat food and drink Champagne with the hottest woman that was there?”

“ Oh, No…Cheesy pick up line!!!”

We both laughed.

“That was not…ok, maybe it was cheesy, but I did mean it. I’m a little attracted to you Alexis. In case you haven’t figured it out yet.”

“ A little huh?”

“ Any further information will only be divulged with my attorney present”, I said.

“ Whatever”, Alexis said rolling her eyes and smiling. “I’m attracted to you too Mr. Woodward. Even though you probably have 6 or 7 women panting around the country.”

“ Six or seven is so last year!”

Alexis turned quickly, mouth hanging open, as I began to laugh.

“I’m only kidding”, I added. “I don’t have the time for that kind of stuff. You on the other hand have got to have your own stable of groupies, uh…I mean admirers.”

" No. Nothing like that. My last relationship fizzled out about a year ago. Seems he needed to have more than one woman at a time, thinking that they were his only one."

" Hmm…the playa type dude. Hold that thought as I go get our food."

We pulled into the parking lot of the restaurant and one of the valets opened the rear door for me to exit. It was only a short wait inside, before the waitress returned with our order. The restaurant manager came out to greet me and we talked briefly before I excused myself. When I returned to the limousine, Alexis had removed her shoes and was lying comfortably in the corner of the vehicle. I sat next to her, placing the food bags on the bar and Alexis snuggled in close to me.

" You don't mind, do you", she asked, "I'm kind of exhausted mentally."

"Of course not. Are you kidding me?"

Barry pulled off and we headed for her apartment. It had been a long day, but even though we were both a little tired, we were not ready for the night to end. The short drive was shared in silence. Simply the pulse of our heartbeats creating a soft noise that only the two of us were privy to.

" Want to come up for a while and eat with me", she asked as we pulled into the driveway of her apartment complex?

" Definitely", I replied casually.

Barry parked the car near the building and got out to open our door. Stepping out, I told him I would call him when I was ready. We entered the building and took the elevator up to the upper floors that held her apartment. As we entered, Alexis again removed her shoes and lit a few candles in the living room. She came over to me and took the food bags into the kitchen. A few moments later she returned with the hot food. Placing it on the coffee table and returning to the kitchen to grab a bottle of champagne from the refrigerator. She sat on the floor, resting her body against the couch cushions.

" Join me", she said.

I slid off the couch and onto the floor next to her. Opening the bottle of Champagne, I poured Alexis a glass and then poured one for myself.

We sat in her apartment; Moonlight glistening through her windows, scented candles throughout the living room. There were chairs of course. A Big cushiony couch as well, but we seemed to feel more comfortable for some reason, sitting on the thick carpeted floor, sipping champagne and eating our food.

Alexis had placed the steamed whitefish, mixed vegetables, rice and schezuan chicken on plates before she returned to the living room. We sat, laughing at some of the day's events and reliving some of the better moments. Alexis was even more relaxed now that her fashion show was over and had gone well.

" You have a beautiful apartment Alexis", I said continuing to eat.

"Thank you", she replied.

As I ate, I suddenly became aware that Alexis was not laughing anymore. There was no sound other than the soft music playing in the background, and a gentle breeze blowing in through the window, off the balcony.

I looked up to see Alexis staring at me.

" Am I missing something", I finally asked.

Alexis merely shook her head, no, as she continued to look. Taking a deep breath, she reached into her plate of steamed fish with her chopsticks and lifted a small, bite size, chunk off the plate. Her arm, extended towards me with the morsel, grazing my lower lip with it. I opened my mouth slightly, accepting the small bit of her food.

" You have a strong appetite. That sometimes transfers to other areas as well", she said.

She reached for another bite, only momentarily taking her eyes off of me and bringing another bite to my mouth. Staring intently at my lips and tongue as she quietly fed me pieces of the steamed fish with her chopsticks.

Our eyes met and there was a question in them as she pulled her bottom lip under the upper. Running her tongue across it.

The look on her face could have melted an iceberg as she looked at me. My restraint was no match for my desire as I closed the small distance between us. Slowly kissing her lips. Those tantalizing lips, I had not been able to get off of my mind since our first kiss, last night.

Kissing her again, our tongues moved of their own volition. Colliding against each other in a dance of passion.

A passion that was intensifying. I pulled Alexis closer to me. Hungrily tasting her lips. She returned the passion, moving her hand to the back of my head. Her hands moved from there to the inside of my jacket. Unbuttoning my shirt as we continued to kiss.

My lips moved to her neck and she breathed in deeply as I nibbled on the sensitive area. Reluctantly Alexis pulled away from me. Staring into my eyes.

“ We need to slow this down a little”, she said. I pulled back a little, my hand still resting against her waist.

“ Corey, don’t get the wrong impression. I already like you a lot and that is not exactly like me to fall into lust and like this quickly.”

“ I understand. I don’t want you to do anything that you don’t want to. There’s something that just feels right about us. Its almost like fate.”

“Its not that I don’t want to do this, the problem is…” Her voice trailed off as she kissed me again. This time with a lot more urgency. When the kiss broke, Alexis stood up and reached her hand out to me.

“ The problem is that I do want to do this.”

“ Why don’t we just hold each other and when you’re really ready, I’ll be ready.”

Alexis kissed me again.

“ Come on”, she said taking my hand into hers and leading me into the bedroom.

Once there, we began kissing again. Slowly backing our way towards the bed.

I could still hear the music playing in the living room, bedroom door slightly ajar and the moonlight streaming in through her windows. The moonlight caused an ebony glow throughout the room. She lowered herself onto the mattress, scooting backwards as I joined her. Removing my shirt on the way. I pulled her close to me. Embracing her and kissing her lips, her neck, cheeks.

She returned each kiss, nibbling my ears and rubbing the back of my head.

CHAPTER IX

Morning came almost too quickly. After the hour long, make out session and all night cuddling, I was surprised I didn't wake up with blue balls. We had decided to wait, just a little longer and fell asleep in each other's arms.

Fortunately, I remembered Barry last night and sent him on his way with instructions to pick me up in the morning before Alexis and I fell asleep. .

As the sun peeked into the windows at Alexis' apartment, still holding her close to me I kissed her forehead. Staring out of the window at the Detroit River. Her head lying on my bare chest. Arms wrapped around me, hands beginning to trace little circles on my body.

" Good morning", I said to her.

She stretched her body, pushing herself against me, even more, and then re-wrapping her arms around me.

"Morning."

" Sleep well", I asked?

" Too good. Like a baby."

" That's a good thing right?"

" That is a very good thing. I hope you realize that I don't make a habit of sleeping with someone on the first date."

" Well, Actually this would have been our second date", I reminded her.

" Oh yeah. You mean we could have had sex last night and I could have told everyone that at least I didn't sleep with you on the first date? Man!! Missed opportunities", She proclaimed smiling.

" Well, you know the date isn't really over", I smiled

" Nope. Too Late! The mood is gone", she teased.

" I'm a day late and a dollar short, always", I replied.

Alexis just smiled and cuddled more.

" Don't worry, Mr. Woodward. If you make it that far, it will be worth the wait."

“ If…?”

At that moment, there was a knock on the bedroom door and it flung open at the same time.

“ Rise and shine party girl”, Katie said walking into the room.

Suddenly realizing that Alexis was not alone, Katie froze, mouth open and eyes widening.

“ I’m sorry, I didn’t realize,” she stammered.

“I’m going to step back out now.”

Katie said retreating to the living room, closing the door behind her.

“ That might be a good idea”, Alexis said laughing a little.

“ Good morning Katie”, I called after her.

“Oh my God”, Alexis added. Placing her head into her hands and burying herself against my chest.

“ Katie has a key huh.”

We both laughed.

“ I kind of forgot about that. This is also my office and she is here to work”, Alexis said.

" So I have to do the morning after, walk of shame", I questioned, chuckling and shaking my head.

" Well you could always hide here in my bedroom until she leaves. Who knows what could happen on lunch break", she teased.

I simply gave her a funny look, as if to say, "Yeah right" and then got up from the bed.

I had only removed my shirt, socks and shoes, as we had only cuddled throughout the night. I figured I would call for Barry, head home and shower and then begin the day.

Alexis got up from the bed and walked over to where I was retrieving my shirt from a chair in her room.

" I take it that is a no", she said smiling.

" It is more like, we both have things to do today and missing you, thinking of you all day could turn into something by tonight."

" Clever save, Mr. Woodward", she said smiling and wrapping her arms around my waist. We shared a light kiss.

" Never, ever, tell a woman no. Especially me", she said smiling. "I'll be right back", she stated, giving me another kiss and heading for the living room.

" Uh...No", I said as she reached the door. She looked back and smiled.

Katie was busying herself at a computer in the dining area checking email. She looked up as Alexis approached with a smile and look of disbelief on her face.

Alexis looked at her blushing a bit. The unasked question lingered briefly in the air.

" Nothing happened Bitch", she laughed. "At least not yet."

" Uh huh. Sure it didn't", Katie looked back nodding her head.

" We came back here after the show, had a couple of drinks and cuddled."

" That's it? "

"That's it."

" You disappoint me Alexis. I would have fucked his brains out", Katie said looking serious and turning back to the computer.

Alexis looked at her with her mouth open, feigning shock and both broke into laughter. I walked into the living room as they were giggling.

“ Well. It couldn’t be my performance”, I said adjusting my suit jacket.

“ Good morning Corey”, Katie greeted me.

“ Good morning Katie. I’m going to let you ladies continue with, uh, whatever you were discussing and I will see you both tonight at my grand opening”, I smiled.

“ Sounds good”, Katie said.

Alexis pouted.

“I suppose I can let you leave. I was going to hold you captive, but there would probably be a few people disappointed if you didn’t show.”

“ Maybe one or two”, I said smiling.

Alexis and I walked towards the door.

“See you later Katie”, I said.

“ Bye Corey.”

Alexis gave me a light kiss, then pulled back reluctantly.

" I'll see you later"; I smiled and gave her another light kiss.

" Call me later. Let me know how the day is going."

" I will", I said turning and walking out of the door.

Alexis closed the door and walked back into the dining area where Katie was sitting.

" I suppose that I should knock and then wait a minute from now on", Katie joked.

Alexis looked back at her with a smug look, biting her lip slightly, reacting to Katie's sarcastic remark, she laughed slightly.

"That might be a good idea", She finally replied.

Both women laughed.

" I'm hitting the shower, I'll be out in a minute", Alexis said walking towards the bedroom.

" Good idea, you smell like guilt", Katie ribbed!

Alexis kept walking, but raised her hand with her middle finger extended.

CHAPTER X

By the time I had taken the elevator down to the first floor and walked out of the door, Barry had returned and was waiting for me. How he got from Bloomfield Hills to downtown Detroit that quickly, I didn't even want to know. The car seemed intact so I didn't worry about it.

Barry stepped out of the vehicle as I approached and opened the door.

"Good morning Mr. Woodward", he said. " I trust you had a good night."

" A very good night, Barry. Looking forward to today and another very good night", I smiled and got into the limousine.

Barry closed the door and then returned to the drivers seat.

" Need to go to the house for a while and get prepared for the day and then down to the hotel and greet our guest."

" Yes sir, Mr. Woodward", He replied and put the car into motion.

I leaned into the cushions and dialed Kenny on my cell.

He picked up on the first ring.

" What up Kenny?"

" Everything's ready. Sound check at 3pm. YJ is at the hotel and staff arriving at 4pm for last minute instructions and inspection."

" Dude, you have got to be the smoothest general manager alive. I'm on my way to the house for a minute and then I will stop off at the hotel and say hey, to those guys. Then I will be at the club", I offered.

"Put your feet up big homey. We got this." Kenny replied.

" Alright man. I'll see you a little later."

"Bet."

As we hung up the phone, I relaxed a little more as the events of last night replayed itself in my mind. I think we probably made out for about a half hour before we figured we had better stop and just let the days exhaustion, lull us into a peaceful sleep. A half hour after that we actually did stop and go to sleep. It felt good to hold Alexis in my arms like that. It felt even better to wake up with her still in the same position, drawing imaginary circles on my chest. Dating, a friend with benefits, one-night stands. It was all beginning to get pretty old. Having money, respect and a modicum of power really only completed part of life's circle. Having someone to share it with, that was an equal, was the other half. Alexis held that potential.

Only time would tell what was in store with our budding romance.

I needed to grab a shower and change clothes, then head over to the hotel, so that I could be a gracious host. I was looking forward to doing business with YJ on a continuous basis.

At present his new single was number 2 on the hot singles charts. His album was number 5 with a bullet. Meaning it was a hot product and was expecting to go up.

YJ was the hottest rapper out right now, as could be attested to by the brainwash rotation of his video on all of the cable music stations.

This would be his first Michigan appearance and I managed to outbid the larger promotion companies to get this appearance, partly because we were old friends from the block. That's how you do it, when you stay in the streets.

A few phone conversations later, Barry pulled the limousine into my driveway. A quick shower and we would be out again. I sprinted up the stairs, into the bedroom and into my closet, where I pulled out an ice white Sean John Track suit and laid it on the bed. Going over to my dresser, I pulled some socks and boxers out, threw them to the bed and headed for the shower.

I was finally getting excited about my grand opening. I turned on the radio and heard the commercials that had been blasting all week for my grand opening.

As I let the water heat up in the shower WTRB did a 3 in a row mix of YJ. A song from his new album, followed by one of his guest appearances on another artist' song and finally his latest single to be released from his debut album.

As I listened to the lyrics, I couldn't help, but make that screw face. This cat was so lyrically fire it was undeniable.

I quickly finished my shower, listening to the radio and the hype being created about tonight. I was now wide-awake, excited and feeling good.

I dressed hurriedly, spraying on some cologne and grabbing one of my watches from a case on my dresser. The diamond encased Jacob. Might as well meet YJ on his own playing field, I laughed to myself. I also grabbed my long diamond chain, tossed it onto my neck and headed for the door. Strapping my watch around my wrist as I walked quickly. Once in the limo, I called YJ's cell phone.

He picked it up on the 5th ring and I could hear his entourage in the background.

" What up playboy", I said into the phone.

“ What up Corey? Where you at man? We getting ready to have breakfast down here at the hotel.”

“ I’m actually on my way down there.”

“ Alright man. Hit me when you get closer. We gonna figure out which one of these restaurants down here we want to hit. So when you call, I’ll let you know where we are.”

“Bet. See you guys in a few minutes.”

“ Going to the Athenaeum Barry”, I told my driver.

“ Yes sir.”

Barry pulled back out onto the road and we were in the streets once again.

CHAPTER XI

" Alexis Marie, may I help you", Katie answered as the phone at Alexis' office rang.

"Hey Katie, What's up? This is Sophie."

" Hey girl, what's up?"

" Is the fashion mogul up and about yet?

" She's up all right. She might have even been up all night, but she won't go into any details. Maybe you can drag it out of her", said Katie and Sophie laughed.

" You are getting real close to stepping outside Missy", Alexis smiled as she hit the speakerphone switch in front of Katie.

"What's up Soph?"

" Hey Lex", so how did it go last night?"

" I assume you are talking about Mr. Woodward dropping me off at home", Alexis said coyly.

Katie made a choking sound

"Sorry", Katie said.

Alexis gave her an evil look, knowing that Sophie heard it.

"I take it by Katie's noise, that there is a little more to it and yes, I am talking about him dropping you off. Spill the beans girl, don't keep us all in suspense."

" There is not a lot to tell", He did spend the night, but he was a perfect gentlemen and just cuddled with me all night."

" What? Alexis he is a single, rich and handsome man and you are single as well, this is about your third, or fourth date. I would have fucked his brains out."

" I told her the same thing", Katie joined in laughing.

" The two of you are incorrigible", Alexis whined as they all laughed!

" We made out, does that help?"

" Partially redeeming Lex", Sophie said sarcastically.

" Well, a girl must do what a girl must do." added Katie.

" So you are going to the grand opening tonight right?"

"Yeah, I'm dragging Katie's party pooper butt to it", Alexis said.

"Hey! I am not a party pooper", Katie protested.

" Well, I guess I will see you two in VIP."

" Yeah, I'll probably get there about 7:30 or 8:00", said Alexis.

" You're not going for the dinner reception?"

" Oh. What time does that start?"

" At 5", said Sophie.

"Okay. Maybe we'll go ahead and plan to meet you guys over there at 5 then."

"Alright then see you there. Bye you two."

" Ok Soph, see you then", Alexis said.

" See you later Sophie", Katie said hanging up the phone.

" Is it formal or casual", Katie inquired.

" Casual", Alexis replied looking at the flyer from her purse. " I almost forgot I had this."

" Must have been all of that Champagne and kissing", Katie joked.

“ Ha ha”, Alexis added. “ I’m going to get dressed.”

Alexis headed back to the bedroom to get ready as Katie continued with the e-mails and phone calls for the day.

CHAPTER XII

Hanging out with YJ and his entourage was cool, but I had a restaurant and nightclub to run. It was getting late, so I told the guys that I would send a car for them at about 2:30 and that I would see them at the club. I left and made it over to The Playground, so we could open the doors for 5pm dinner.

Kenny and the staff were all ready to go when I got there. Candles lit on each table and soft background music playing.

This was to me almost the equivalent of having a child. Two years of planning and construction went into this day. Advance promotion, VIP cards, DVD invites for the opening and flying out food critics and reporters. All of it culminating in today's extravaganza.

With YJ's sound check out of the way and he and his crew back at the hotel, it was simply wait for dinner; pray that there would be people to show up and then hopefully impress them with our service and food. Nervous was not the word to describe how I felt.

As the clock struck 5 pm, I opened the doors and the crowd that had gathered in front of the building began to file in. There were gasps and smiles as the customers entered the dining area of the building. Comments of beautiful and fabulous were overheard as the Maitre D and I were greeting people at the door and Kenny pulled double duty, greeting people and making sure everything was running smoothly from the waitresses to the kitchen.

As the first orders were being taken and brought back to the kitchen, I saw Paul and Sophie coming towards the entrance.

“ Congratulations Core”, Paul said as he reached out to shake my hand.

“ Congratulations Corey”, Sophie added as she hugged me and kissed my cheek.

“ Thanks you two.

For the record Paul, I am now excited”, I said as we all got a chuckle out of that remark.

" The place looks wonderful Corey", Sophie added.

" As long as the chef's don't poison anybody, I think we're good", I said knocking on the wood banister.

" Whatever dude. I'm ordering steak. You got any lobsters and champagne up in this piece?"

" All right Money Bagels. Let me have Shawn seat you two, so I can get all your loot", I said laughing.

" Its all yours my friend. I'm proud of you Corey and I can't wait for the YJ concert later."

"Prepare to do a lot of sweating", Sophie said.

" I'm ready to dance all night."

" We'll dance all night, alright", Paul said kissing her on the forehead. " Alright Corey, we're going to go get some of this delicious food."

I informed Shawn that these were VIP guests as he returned

Sophie and Paul followed Shawn the Maitre' D, to the dining area as I returned to greeting the guests as they filed in.

After a few moments, I saw Alexis and Katie coming towards the door.

Alexis looked as if she were attending the academy awards with the dress she wore.

She was absolutely stunning.

"Hey Corey", Katie said as they approached.

" Hey Katie."

" Hello again, Mr. Woodward", Alexis said staring into my eyes.

" You are gorgeous", I said. She smiled and gave me a hug and light kiss on the lips.

" I hope your staff is ready. Katie and I are ordering everything on the menu", she said.

" You haven't seen our menu. That means you will be spending a lot of time here", I laughed.

The ladies were both laughing as Shawn returned from seating the customers before them. I spoke to him in French and told him to escort the ladies to the VIP area.

" VIP, Mr. Woodward, I'm flattered", Alexis said.

" I should have gathered that you spoke French. Next time I'll try Mandarin", I laughed.

Alexis muttered, Try again, sexy in Chinese as her and Katie followed Shawn to the VIP area. Katie tried to cover up her laugh as I shook my head in defeat.

I greeted a few more guests and then joined my friends in the VIP area. As I sat down next to Alexis, one of my waiters approached and asked if I would like a glass of champagne.

"Definitely", I said as he poured a glass for me.

" Looks like success partner", Paul said as I turned towards them.

" The food is delicious Corey", Sophie added.

" Its really beautiful Corey and I love this atmosphere", Alexis said.

"Thank you all, but there is even more to come."

" Well if this is any indication of how this place is going to be, you have a hit. Damn, The rich get richer", Paul said.

Everyone laughed.

" Whatever, dude. I heard the rumor about your private jet."

" That would be your private jet sir. Don't twist this around trying to hide."

" No jets for me thanks", I added laughing. "Besides, its not really, "My" jet.

The evening continued with me answering a few questions to reporters, greeting food critics and taking pictures and before you knew it, it was 8pm and time for the concert.

The lights in the building dimmed slowly and I stood up at the balcony of the VIP area.

A follow spotlight was aimed at me and an assistant brought me a wireless microphone.

" I would like to thank all of you for making our opening day a fantastic success. I hope you are all enjoying yourselves as much as I have so far."

Everyone applauded.

"Without further delay, I would like to introduce to you all, one of my really good friends. Platinum recording artist, YJ"

Everyone began applauding wildly, as YJ told his Deejay to drop it. The music boomed from the P.A. system as the stage lights began to circulate.

Y.J entered the stage and the crowd erupted as he started to perform his hit single.

YJ was a very talented artist and he had the music world on stranglehold right now, with his music and his street buzz. I was very fortunate to get him for my grand opening and even more fortunate to count him as one of my friends.

His performance was dynamic and engaging and by the time it was over, I was exhausted as were many others. I made my way to the backstage area to congratulate him and to introduce him to Sophie, Paul, Alexis and Katie.

He was just toweling off as we approached him backstage.

" I've got to have you back, my dude", I said.

" Anytime Core", he said. " I hope you guys have got some food left in this place", he joked.

" I'm sure we can microwave you something", I countered laughing.

" You got jokes", YJ laughed.

" I'll make sure you guys get taken care of", I said shaking hands and giving a hug to his Deejay and to his hype man.

" Thanks Core."

I walked with my friends back to the front of the restaurant.

" What's up for the rest of the night Corey", Paul asked.

" Counting money", I laughed. " Not sure really. Have to make sure everything is everything with Kenny and then probably back to Bloomfield. Get ready to do it all over again."

“ Gee, You brought in probably about a hundred grand tonight and you are going to be burdened with doing it again tomorrow, your life sucks Corey”, Paul joked shaking his head.

“ Get out”, I said smiling and pointing at the door!

Everyone laughed.

“We’ll see you tomorrow Corey”, Sophie said giving me a hug and kiss. Paul gave me a hug, as did Katie. Alexis moved forward to say goodbye and I stopped her.

“ What are you doing tonight, pretty lady?”

“ What would you like me to do”, she said?

“ I would like you to stay with me”, I said.

“ Then I suppose that is what I am doing tonight” she replied inches from me.

“ Katie, I’m going to stay here. You can take my car and Corey will give me a ride back and I’ll see you on Monday”, she said handing her the keys to her car.

“ Ok. You kids have a great weekend”, she said.

“ Thanks. Bye Katie”, I said.

" See you Kates", Alexis said. Katie made a gesture to Alexis when I turned my head, but I caught it out of the corner of my eye, for her to call her. When I turned back, I invited her to the restaurants office so we could close up shop and get out of there.

Kenny came back to the office with the day's receipts and he and I went over everything. After depositing opening money into the safe, he put a deposit bag together and left for the night depository with a guard. Tomorrow there would be a regular pick-up started with an armored car service. Good thing I trusted Kenny. He walked out of the front door with almost $50,000 in cash.

"Now Miss Parkhurst, what do I do with you", I said walking over to where she was standing. I placed a hand on each side of her waist and kissed her. Her arms came up to encircle my neck as she returned my kiss.

" That will do for a start", she said as the kiss broke.

" Let's get out of here", I said, turning off the lights and walking hand in hand with her to the front door. I punched in the alarm code and we stepped out of the door. Barry was already waiting by the curb as we exited.

Once inside of the vehicle, I instructed him to take us around the park and he set the car into motion. Heading for Belle Isle.

Belle Isle was a small island owned by the city on the Detroit River. It was just off of Jefferson Avenue, downtown Detroit and regularly played host to the Boat races, Detroit Grand Prix and a host of other events, picnics and just general cruising.

I remembered as a teenager, bringing my dates here or just hanging out with friends.

Sometimes I would come here alone and sit at the band shell to clear my head. I came to think about life and all of my dreams, as well.

It had literally been years since I had done that, but tonight it seemed like just the thing to do.

Alexis cuddled into me as we sipped glasses of champagne, with her back resting against my chest. The sunroof was open and we gazed at the stars through the roof of the car, soft music playing on the stereo.

The moonlight just seemed right as Alexis turned towards me, placed a hand on my cheek and kissed me. It was almost a magical glow throughout the interior of the limousine.

Putting my glass down, I responded by running my hands over her curves. Gently but firmly pulling her closer to me. I wanted to consume this woman. I wanted to be a part of her soul.

I broke our kiss momentarily to hit the intercom switch.

" Let's go home Barry", I said.

" Yes, sir", he replied.

I switched the intercom off and returned to Alexis. Running my fingers into her hair, our tongues writhing against each other.

She moved to straddle me, kissing my neck and cheek and then returning to my lips.

We continued throughout the drive back to West Bloomfield, our passion mounting.

As Kenny pulled into the driveway, we reluctantly parted, straightening our clothes, with me trying to adjust a very visible erection.

Barry opened the rear door, cautiously and we exited.

" Goodnight Barry", I told him.

" Goodnight Barry", Alexis joined.

" Goodnight Mr. Woodward, Goodnight Miss Parkhurst."

Barry closed the door and re-entered the driver's seat as Alexis and I made our way into the house. Once the door shut, our kisses restarted. Pulling each other closely, tugging at clothes as we backed our way towards the couch.

" Uh uh", I breathed. "Upstairs."

Taking her hand, I led her to the staircase leading to the upper levels.

I let her go first and patted her butt as she walked up the stairs. When we reached the top floor, I directed her into my bedroom

Pulling Alexis close to me, I met with no resistance as I unzipped her dress.

Her hands were occupied with my belt and pants zipper. We removed all of each other's clothing hurriedly, desperately and fell onto the king size mattress.

Our hands were moving and exploring everywhere at once. As I shifted positions her legs wrapped around my body. She pulled me closer into her and then there was the precious moment when we united.

CHAPTER XIII

In a private airport, just outside of the city, Amanda Woodward's chartered plane set down. She had missed her commercial flight, and thus missed her brother's grand opening. Not wanting to wait for the make-up flight, she simply used some hours from her brother's private jet account as he told her; she could, anytime she needed

Two hours later she was on a plane heading for Detroit. Had she waited, she would not have gotten into town until the next day. As it stood, with her missing the opening and then not being able to get hold of Corey when she arrived, she might as well have stayed and waited for the commercial plane. When she touched down, she called one of her girlfriends to pick her up from the terminal, figuring that Corey must have his phone off and then went to her apartment. She had spent the last two weeks in Florida working on a new project for her boss and was back home to her not so normal life.

Not so normal, because she had become Ill in Florida. Something in the air she thought, maybe a flu bug or something, a virus. All she really knew was that one day in the bathroom, she was coughing up blood and the next day, she was fine. She would make an appointment and go see her regular doctor in a couple of days. She was sure it had something to do with being run down and the change in climates. After all, most of her family suffered with sinus problems and a couple of times a year, these same types of things happened. She had no reason to believe anything else. Her friend, Melissa came inside with her, helping to take her luggage up to her place. Once in the apartment, the two ladies sat down to relax.

“ Thanks again, Melissa, I couldn’t get hold of Corey all day.”

“ He probably was just really occupied with his grand opening”, Melissa replied.

“ Probably. My brother is such a workaholic.”

“ Well, I’m going to get back to the city, give me a call when you’re settled tomorrow.”

“ Thanks again, Melissa, see you.”

“ Goodnight”, Melissa said as she exited the apartment.

Amanda was positive that Corey wouldn’t be especially mad, but more disappointed that she had not made it to the grand opening. She would call him in the morning and apologize profusely, while making sure she made it into the restaurant that night.

Amanda turned on her stereo, ran some bath water and turned the sheets and comforter down on her bed. A quick bath and a good night sleep would do her good, she thought. Tomorrow was a brand new day and she had plenty to accomplish in it.

A report to her boss at the advertisement and promotions company where she worked, checking in with her brother and getting over to his restaurant, going through the stack of mail that had collected while she was away, grocery shopping…

She needed a vacation, she thought and it damn well would not be Florida. Her two-week assignment there originally sounded like paradise. Fun in the sun, make sure the client was happy and hit some A-list parties at night. Unfortunately the best laid plans of mice, men and women prove otherwise more often than not.

From the moment her plane touched down in South Beach it was non-stop running. Getting product samples in, sending press releases and doing follow up, organizing the drink girls, interviewing models at their agencies, at the clubs, at poolside, at the hotel…

A good scream would be nice here, Amanda thought amusing her self.

CHAPTER XIV

Alexis was slightly disoriented when she awoke the next morning with my arm around her waist. After figuring out where she was, her first thoughts were to crawl out from under my arm and freshen up in the bathroom before I woke up.

" Good morning", I whispered.

" Good morning", she said realizing it was too late. She relaxed a little and cuddled closer against me.

"Sleep well?"

" I think you knocked out all of the tension in my body."

"Ditto", I chuckled.

" You have a show tonight, right?"

"That I do ma'am."

" What do you have for the rest of the day?"

" Breakfast, making love to you, lunch, making love to you again, shower, get dressed, check in with tonight's act, a quickie with you in the limo, dinner, the show, and finally make love to you all night."

" Sounds like a plan, however Mr. Woodward, I have a meeting with my sales team this afternoon."

" Oops, did I forget that you have a life too, my bad, it was very unintentional."

" So let's change the plan to breakfast", she paused, "After we make love."

She turned towards me, burying her face against my neck as she wrapped her arms around me.

" Mmmm", I said kissing her neck. " I love the way you think."

Alexis returned my kisses on my neck and chest and melted into me once again. This morning there was not the frenzied and passionate rush as there was last night, but slow and purposeful.

Learning the things that made each other's bodies respond.

What touches, did what combined with what kisses, licks or tickles.

Last night was more like, “we fucked”.
This morning, we made love and when it was all said and done, we lay there almost falling asleep again, before I remembered that Louisa should be showing up any minute.

“ What would you like for breakfast”, I asked?

“ Hmm, are you cooking for me?”

“ Not exactly. My housekeeper and cook should be arriving any minute.”

“ You have a cook?”

“ Its not that I can’t cook myself, it’s just that normally I am so tied up with other things that I don’t feel like it. We won’t even get into housecleaning.”

“ I was going to ask you, what woman was doing your cleaning here”, things looked a bit neat for a heterosexual male bachelor.”

“ Ha ha”, I said. “So what would you like?”

“ What are you having?”

“ Probably an omelet. Louisa makes the most fantastic omelets. I love em’ with three chesses, sausage, mushrooms, onions, green peppers, tomatoes and red jalapenos”

“ Sounds delicious”, I’ll have the same except without the jalapeños”

“ Not into spicy foods huh?”

“ You’re all the spice, I can handle for right now, thank you”, she laughed.

“ I’m grabbing a shower”, I said getting up from the bed.

“ I’ll meet you there”, she replied with a seductive look.

I smiled and headed for the bathroom. After turning on the water and letting it heat, Alexis did in fact join me. We finished and stepped out and I heard the kitchen door opening. I grabbed a towel and playfully swatted Alexis on the butt as I headed for the bedroom and my robe.

“ Can I borrow a T-shirt”, she asked?

“Of course, Inside of my closet, there is a chest of drawers. Top, left hand side is where you will find Tee’s. I’ll meet you downstairs. Still know the way?”

“ I think I can find it.”

" Many have tried, many have gotten lost", I joked.

" …And just how many is many", Alexis said with an accusatory look.

" I'm kidding, I'm kidding", I replied.

Alexis had a "yeah right" type of look on her face, but continued towards the closet.

I went downstairs to the kitchen.

" Good morning Louisa", I said entering the kitchen.

" Good morning Mr. Woodward"

" Louisa, I have a guest this morning."

" Will the two of you be having breakfast today?"

" Yes. Could you make two of your fantastic omelets? Mine will be the usual and hers will be the usual minus the jalapenos."

" Be ready in just a few moments", Louisa said.

Alexis padded downstairs to the kitchen.

" Louisa, this is Alexis Parkhurst, Alexis, this is Louisa."

" How are you Madame", Louisa asked?

" Fantastic. Beautiful to meet you Louisa."

" Breakfast will be ready in just a moment."

" We'll be in the living room Louisa", I said and directed Alexis to the big room.

In the living room, I grabbed the television remote and switched on the cable music station, as Alexis looked at various pictures that adorned the room."

On the mantle above the fireplace she came across a picture of my sons.

"Are these your children", she asked?

" Yes. The youngest one is 18 and the oldest is 20 now. That was taken quite some time ago", I said.

" Well, I would think so, looking at the pictures", she said smiling.

" Where are they now?"

" They live in Florida.

Their mother and I divorced when they were 9 and 11."

" I'm sorry. Do you see them much?"

" I get down to Florida maybe twice a month. I do a little business there and I own an apartment building in Miami."

" What about the Ex?"

" She is in Miami as well. We don't talk very much."

" That's too bad. Ever thought about reconciling?"

" Many times. The distrust and the anger just won't allow us to have any real open conversation. Even if she was the slightest bit interested, which I don't think she is and my interest in it has vacillated back and forth. I still care for her, but she has changed in so many ways. My main thought at first was I didn't want what our divorce was going to do to our children and in addition, I knew that we had misunderstood a lot of things that she and I could have communicated better between ourselves. We were young, is all I can really say", I said sitting on the cushiony couch and lowering the volume of the Television.

" Are you suggesting that she doesn't know how caring and sensitive you are?"

" I believe that she believes, I am a worthless piece of crap, because if she believed for one second that neither of us meant to do the things that we have done to each other, then I can't understand why we didn't just sit down and work it out. If not totally for us, then for our children. In other words, if she didn't believe that, then nothing we have all gone through the last few years makes intelligent sense"

"She has custody?"

"We've always had joint custody. They didn't move to Miami until after my youngest son's 18th Birthday. My oldest was already there."

" What are their names?"

" Alex and Michael."

" It must have been pretty hard on them", she said sitting next to me on the couch.

" Very much so. They lived with me at first and when the divorce was finalized. They moved in with their mother.

I was broken mentally, spiritually and financially. I have had to fight my way back from the dead basically. I lost hundreds of thousands of dollars when we first split, but I made it back."

" I'll say you did", said Alexis. "Your oldest is Alex or your youngest?"

"My youngest."

" If they were living with you, what made you decide to have them live with their mother?"

" It wasn't my choice. The judge decided that since she had some things in place, that I didn't seem to have at the time, that they should go and live with her."

" That must have been very rough on you", Alexis said rubbing my back?

"It is one of the most horrible feelings in the world. Your rights are taken away and you are violated. Everyone around you is acting like, you're overreacting and its being done right in front of the people that are supposed to be trying to make things all right, the ones that are supposed to be trying to assist you. All the while they are saying they are trying to make it better for the kids and they are just guessing. It is never really about the kids anyway. Its about who did what and who gets what. It causes physical reactions. Everything from crying to chest pains, to full, blown panic attacks. Your hands are tied. Your cry for help is muffled, people ridicule you and you have to watch as your children attempt to suck it all up and be strong…and YOU, try to suck it up and be strong, All the while your insides are screaming.

"You make it sound almost like rape", Alexis said to me

I simply looked Alexis square in the eye…

"Yeah", I said, "It does sound a lot like that doesn't it?"

" I'm so sorry that happened to you", she said hugging me.

" Then you wonder if it is merely because I am a man and then you have to wonder if it is because I am a Black man. It was devastating and all I wanted to do was to sit down and make any mistake that I had ever made all right. I would have done anything. Instead, I wound up spiraling down an endless tube and I had to dig my way out of it first emotionally and then financially. At every turn, something tried to block me or knock me back down. Even her, although I don't believe she realized all the time what she was doing."

" Hmm."

" Yeah, I know. Sometimes I wondered if she knew "Exactly" what she was doing as well", I said cracking a sarcastic smile.

" Well, the main thing is that you came through it and your children came through it and you are all living and healthy."

" Albeit a bit emotionally scarred for life, but yeah", I said.

I took a long deep breath. Remembering one of the days that I saw our relationship breaking down. When I saw everything that I had worked for with her and before her, all of my life…ending.

" So have you really moved on with your life", Alexis asked, snapping me back to the present.

" You tell me", I said turning to her and kissing her lips.

" Well, you make love like you have", she said returning my kiss, smiling and staring into my eyes.

" I might just be that good", I smiled.

" ... And so modest too, I tell you", she said sarcastically.

Louisa entered the living room area.

"Excuse me, your breakfast is ready", she said.

" Thank you Louisa", I replied.

" I have everything set in the dining room", she replied going back into the kitchen.

Alexis and I got up from the couch and crossed the living room into the dining room area.

The table was set with omelets, toast, juice and coffee with fresh fruit on the side.

"Yum", Alexis said heading towards the table.

" I'm going to definitely have to steal her, Mr. Woodward."

“ Or just visit a lot”, I said.

“ Hmm, you wish.”

“ Yes I do”, I said.

As we sat down to eat, the house telephone rang. I excused myself to answer it and walked into an adjoining hallway.

It was my sister Amanda.

“ What’s up you? You missed my grand opening”, I said into the phone, then listening to her excuse.

“ I don’t want to hear, well what had happened was…you used my plane account?

Okay. I will see you later tonight… Alright, I Love you”, I said ending the conversation.

I returned to the living room, breakfast and Alexis.

“ Everything okay”, she asked, noticing that I was a little frazzled.

“Yeah, just some family stuff. It will be okay. I just…” my voice trailed off. I didn’t really want to even talk about it. I was a little angry but I just shook my head.

“ It will be fine.” I finally said.

Alexis picked up on my mood change and figured out that whatever was troubling me, I would take care of, so she dropped the subject. The mild curiosity about the “I love you” statement she picked up on was also quelled when I said family. Alexis had been deceived and led on before, so she had become very cautious as time went on.

At this point, they were just hooking up, even though it was obvious to her that she liked him. So pretty much there was nothing to lie about, so she relaxed.

“ Mmm, this omelet is delicious”, she said.

“ A beautiful way to start a friendship”, I said.

With that we continued eating, before Alexis had to leave and start her day and I had to get ready for my evening at the restaurant.

I liked the way Alexis was comfortable in her surroundings and our little night we spent together, and she sure looked cute walking around with her panties and my T-shirt on. Maybe she wanted to leave a mental picture in my mind I thought and if that was the case then she was doing a hell of a job of it. Between that picture and the look on her face when she had an orgasm, I didn't think there was going to be too much that could erase those pictures from my mind. After breakfast, we strolled upstairs to get dressed. However, one kiss led to three, one hug turned into groping and the morning agenda was postponed for a short period of time.

CHAPTER XV

Amanda was finding it hard to breath, let alone stand for some reason. Her heartbeat was racing and she felt dizzy as she walked up the stairs to her apartment.

Maybe lying down for a while would help, she thought to herself. After all it was a very hot day and she had been running around since early morning grocery shopping, picking up laundry, dropping off packages, etc.

When she finally made it to the top of the stairs, she leaned against the door wall for support. Catching her breath, before inserting the key into the lock and letting herself into her apartment. Dragging her bags in, she plopped down in her recliner chair, staring at the ceiling.

"FUCK!!!"

She had forgotten to close the door and there was dread at exerting the energy right now to get up and close it. She mustered the strength, closed the door and plopped back into the chair, enjoying the central air blowing on her and cooling her scorched body.

She found the television remote, after fishing for it on the end table between the sofa and the recliner she sat in and turned it on to a news station.

Her breathing slowly returned to normal as she relaxed, not quite understanding why she was so out of breath. Only thing she could think of was the nasty bump she took, while swimming in Florida. A wave had come in too fast for her to react and pushed her against the sea wall by the hotel. When she got out, she didn't have any bruises, so she dismissed it. Just a few scratches she had thought, but now in the light of recent incidents with her shortness of breath and the blood from her mouth the other night, she wondered if it could possibly be more. She resolved that there would be no playing around on Monday and that she would schedule an immediate appointment to get things checked out.

Before she knew it, as she sat watching television and thinking, she had fell asleep in the chair. Her dreams taking her away to a forgotten paradise filled with white lights and sun.

She was barefoot in the sand, besides clear blue water.

When she awoke it was well past midnight. Groggily she stood up from the chair, a bit drained and cramped from sleeping in an awkward position. How long had she been asleep she wondered. She picked up her grocery bags and walked towards the kitchen, fortunately there had not been anything that needed refrigeration in them.

As she moved into the kitchen, she paused at the microwave.

Staring at the clock, she gasped, realizing that she had missed Corey's for the second night in a row.

" Oh my God", She said defeated, her hand covering her face.

Calling Corey and trying to explain her missing his restaurant two days in a row, was not something that she was looking forward to. She knew it had to be done though. It just was not going to happen right this second.

CHAPTER XVI

It was 2am when Corey received the text from Amanda. He was standing at the riverfront in Hart Plaza with Alexis. Standing behind her, his arms snugly positioned around her waist as they watched the boats go by and the moon play with the gentle rolling of the waves. Corey casually reached to his phone holster and pulled out his phone. Running his finger across the tabs to view his text messages and giving Alexis a reassuring peck on the back of her neck.

Looking at the text message, I couldn't help, but to think "Here we go again." as I read the apology from Amanda. I let out a deep sigh and replaced the phone to my holster.

"Booty Call", Alexis inquired smiling?

" Not even", I said.

She went back to staring at the ships as they were passing by.

“ Corey, if you have to go or something I will understand”, she said.
“ Its just my irresponsible sister, once again standing me up. She was supposed to be at my restaurant opening tonight, trying to make up for yesterday’s standing me up.”
“Wow. Doesn’t sound very responsible. Well, you always have to take things at face value. She may have a legitimate reason for not being able to attend.”
“You don’t know my sister”, I said.
Alexis pulled Corey’s arms closer around her, making him snuggle in a little more.
Leaning her head back onto his shoulder she exhaled, letting go of the mental pressures of the day and relishing in the moment.
“ I want to know you though”, she said.
“ I’m pretty much an open book. Anything you would like to know, just ask me.”
“ I’ll remember to do that”, she said.
Alexis breathed in and exhaled audibly again.

“ This is nice. It’s been a while since I’ve been able to just relax and be romantic with someone.”

“ As gorgeous as you are, it’s only out of choice.”

“ I seem to intimidate some men”, she said.

“ Good. Less competition for me”, I said.

Alexis laughed and turned around, putting her arms around my neck and shoulders.

“ You believe you have to compete for me Mr. Woodward?”

“ I’m a realist, let’s just leave it at that.”

“ Now what does that suppose to mean”, she asked.

“It means that I try not to count my chickens before they are hatched.”

“ I see”, she said leaning her forehead against mine.

I closed the distance between us and gave her a light kiss. Yes Miss Park Hurst. I want to get to know you too, I thought.

" Mmm, I think its time for bed", she murmured.

" Starting to get sleepy huh?"

" No. I just think its time we go to bed", she said and smiled.

I smiled back at her, slowly shaking my head in disbelief.

" Where have you been all of my life", I asked.

Alexis backed away from me and took my hand. Pulling me away from the rivers edge railing.

" Hiding in your wildest dreams", she finally said, smiling.

I laughed.

It was possibly nervous laughter as I realized that her joking comment might be closer to the truth than she realized.

We walked back towards the stairs of Hart Plaza, towards Jefferson Avenue. A saxophonist was playing with a hat on the ground for change.

I stopped as we walked by and reached into my pocket, pulling out a small wad of bills.

When Alexis glanced the other way, I dropped a $20.00 dollar bill into the hat.

He stopped briefly.

"Thank you. God bless", he said and returned to his music.

" You're welcome", I said.

It was a short walk from the plaza, past Cobo Hall and Joe Louis Arena, back to Alexis' apartment, but it was a beautiful night. The kind of night that was made for this type of thing. The moon and stars shining just right. The temperature not too cold or to hot and very beautiful company.

" What have you got to do tomorrow", she asked?

" Supposed to meet Paul at the golf course tomorrow morning early."

" A black man, other than Tiger Woods, that plays golf. Hmmm interesting."

" I kind of play at it. More like Adam Sandler in that Happy Gilmore movie, but it's a good fun, time", I added.

"Besides you haven't lived until you chase some one around on one of those golf carts".

" You are silly", she said placing her hand in my back pocket as we walked.

" What do you have tomorrow?"

" Planning for another fashion show, manufacturing meeting, sales meeting, marketing meeting…" her voice trailed off.

" Sounds like you will be way busier than me tomorrow", I said.

" Of course. Why do you think I'm trying to get some ass tonight?"

I stopped, mid track, laughing.

" You know, you catch me off guard a lot. I'm not used to people being able to surprise me, but I'll tell you, I do like it."

" I haven't made it this far, this quickly by being coy. I'm absolutely sure that you can identify with that."

" Maybe that is why we seem to clique like we do. We understand each other", I said.

" Exactly. Now come on. I want to play heiress and cabana boy", she said smacking my butt.

I shook my head and laughed as I took her hand and we continued walking towards her apartment. Something told me that I was in for a workout.

CHAPTER XVII

The next morning when I finally pulled up in the parking lot of the golf course, Paul was already there unloading his clubs from the back of his Mercedes. Today I was driving my Lexus LS600 as we had been playfully comparing the two vehicles since we saw them at this year's auto show. I bought one, and have been ribbing him on my better gas mileage ever since.

I lowered my passenger window as I pulled up next to him.

"Excuse me caddy, can you get mine next?"

Paul turned around quickly, preparing to go off on whoever had the audacity to call him a caddy and had a mortified look on his face as he saw it was me.

"Ha Ha. Very funny. You're twenty minutes late and about to get your ass kicked. Figuratively and literally", he said.

" Soph, must not have been giving up that ass last night. What's wrong grouchy?"

" Dude, it has just been a hell of a morning and its not even noon yet", he replied.

"What happened", I said getting out of the car and opening my trunk to retrieve my golf bag.

" Sophie and I got into it this morning. It's just a bunch of pressure with trying to get her album done and the marketing, I believe. Then as we are trying to quiet down, my neighbors are knocking on my fucking door, like is everyone alright in there."

"You got to be kidding", I said lowering my golf bag to the ground.

" No. I'm not."

"So what happened?"

" Sophie came to the door and apologized for us making so much noise, probably more so that the neighbor could see that no one was injured or anything."

" You guys were that loud?"

“ So he starts yapping about he was just trying to check things out and in the middle of his little tirade, I slammed the door in his face.”

I laughed, shaking my head at the thought of that sight.

“ So then what happened?”

“ I just went into the kitchen, grabbed my keys and bounced”, said Paul. “ I didn’t want to be around all of that negativity and bull.”

We both picked up our golf bags and headed towards the pro shop, where we could get the keys for one of the golf carts, out behind the pro shop. It looked like it was going to be a beautiful day. Not too hot, but enough sun to keep our deep, dark chocolate tans.

“ Good morning gentlemen”, said the cute attendant behind the counter as we approached.

“Good morning”, I said cheerfully.

“ Yeah. What he said”, Paul added.

I laughed. The attendant merely looked over at Paul after acknowledging my return of her greeting.

" Don't mind him. He just had a really rough morning and knows that now he's about to have a rough time on the course", I said.

"Bah Humbug", Paul said, causing the attendant to giggle slightly.

"Sorry, you are having a bad morning sir, hopefully things go better on the course", she said trying to be friendly.

" Not likely", I added.

" We'll see about that. Loser buys."

"Whatever. I'm always buying."

" …And what does that tell you", Paul quipped back?

" Oh, okay. You actually are going to provide a little life back today. I was going to give you up for lost."

" I refuse to let that knucklehead next door spoil my entire day", said Paul.

" Then it's off to the course. I hope you brought your credit card with you. I'm feeling really, really thirsty. Not to mention that I hear they have an excellent Steak and Lobster dinner here."

“ You will never see it my friend”, he said as we walked out of the back door and placed our bags in the rear of the golf cart.

“You drive”, I said.

“Arrrgh.” Paul added.

“Pull over by the car”, I said.

Paul started up the little golf cart and wheeled over to the rear of my car. I hit the trunk switch and the rear hood opened, revealing a small cooler. I got out and grabbed it. It held a 12 pack of beer and I placed it on the floor of the cart between us. Paul navigated onto the golf course and we were headed for the first hole. When we got to the green, I cracked open a beer. After Paul stopped the cart, I handed the bottle to him, then reached down and opened another one.

“ You want to go first”, Paul, asked?

“ Nah, you go first man. That first drive might help to start getting things off of your mind”, I said

“ Oh gee thanks”, he replied.

We both got out of the cart; Paul grabbed a driver from his golf bag. He then set his tee in the grass and placed a ball on it; Loosening up and positioning himself for his first drive.
After getting into a comfortable position, he concentrated on the ball. His fingers, tightened around the shaft of the golf club. Then without any movement to warn anyone he called four and sent the small white golf ball high into the air, arcing across the big beautiful sky; then descending back to earth. The ball fell within a few feet of the first hole.
“Top that, rookie”, he said.
I took a deep breath and exhaled loudly as I grabbed a driver from my bag. Walking over to the first tee and placing a tee pin in the ground and a ball on top of it. I took a look at Paul who was smirking confidently on the sidelines. I steadied myself and swung.
“Four”, I called.
The ball made a stunning pirouette against the morning sky. Paul watched intently as the ball began its descent towards the flag. He knew I

was going to be close and the confident look began to give way with every second and then for Paul, the unfathomable. My golf ball dropped, just inches from the 1st hole and rolled into the cup.

Paul stood with his mouth open.

" Looks like the start of a good day", I said as I walked towards the golf cart.

Paul just stared in disbelief and then shook his head.

" You have got to be one of the luckiest bastards that has ever lived. A hole in one", he proclaimed exasperated.

I chuckled, placing my golf club back into the bag and getting into the cart.

" Time's a wasting", I said smiling.

" I sincerely hate you. I just want you to know that", he said walking over to the cart and getting in.

Paul put the vehicle in motion as we headed for the first hole for him to finish up.

" You go out with Lex last night", he inquired?

" Yeah, she came by the restaurant and watched the act and then we went for a walk after closing."

" You guys went for a walk at 2am?"

" A very romantic walk, as a matter of fact."

Paul turned his head suddenly and looked at me.

"You hit that didn't you?"

" A gentlemen never tells", I said.

" Which means that you're safe. So start talking", he said.

I laughed.

"This is the third night we have spent together, nosy neighbor."

"As I said. You have got to be the luckiest bastard alive", he said shaking his head.

" In this particular case, I would have to agree with you my friend. Alexis is fantastic. I really like her. She's smart, funny and all the things a man could ask for in a woman, but you already knew that."

" Yeah. Her and Sophie and I have been friends for years."

“ We’re supposed to get together later on tonight. What are you and Sophie doing?”

“ I don’t know yet. We’re not recording tonight, I don’t think, so it’s pretty much up in the air.”

“ Well, why don’t we all get together and do something”, I offered?

“ Sounds good to me. Let me holler at the little woman, when I redeem myself on this golf course.”

“ Come on Paul! That will take forever”, I laughed.

“ Nah, I’ll just be a minute with her.”

“ I was referring to redeeming yourself on the golf course!”

“ Ha ha. Very funny, very funny. The first shot was 90% luck.”

“ Wow! At least you gave me some credit.”

“ Not really the other 10% was divine intervention”, he chuckled.

“ You are really going to make me finish embarrassing you today, aren’t you?”

" Yada, yada, yada", he said as we pulled up on the first hole.

I got out and retrieved my ball from the hole as Paul went over to his ball with a putter.

" Don't take all day", I joked.

Paul steadied himself and quietly putted the ball into the hole. He turned around to look at me and I yawned.

He screwed up his face, when I did that and grabbed his ball out of the first hole.

This was going to be a long day for him, I thought. I was feeling in too good of a mood.

We set up to play the next hole and Paul muttered something about luck as he prepared to drive his ball toward the second hole.

"Four", he yelled as he let fly.

Unfortunately for Paul, my good mood and my joking threat that he was going to be buying drinks and dinner when it was all over, was almost like prophecy.

I had the best day of golf that I have ever had in my life.

As the last hole was played, with Paul tallying up our scores, I ribbed him with " I had worked up an appetite", " Maybe he should just try dropping the ball in the hole" and my personal favorite a 20% off coupon for golf lessons that I found in the cart

"Let's call the girls and go have a drink at the Bar", I suggested.

" I'm wit it. Maybe Soph will have calmed down a little by now.

CHAPTER XVIII

Paul felt the waters out, by text messaging Sophie his apology and request for a make up drink with Alexis and I, before calling her on the phone to confirm the details.

I couldn't imagine what a fight with Alexis would be like. One thing for sure, I wasn't trying to find out too soon. Of course it is inevitable in any type of relationship, but there was no guarantee that this wonderful feeling they were experiencing together was going to last into a full-blown relationship. At least not yet, it wasn't.

Alexis and Katie were hard at work when Corey called. They had spent the morning creating invoices for the orders they had received at the fashion show and fielding calls from stores and reporters. Alexis had been in one meeting after another today and the chaos didn't look like it was going to end, anytime soon, but it was going to end.

It was going to cease and become non-existent, the minute Corey Woodward pulled up.

Alexis had neglected herself long enough after her break up with Lew and this time she was determined to dance as if no one was watching. Corey was fun. He represented a good time, a really good time. In and out of bed and she wasn't going to let her normal workaholic ways fuck this budding little friendship up.

She liked the way his deep voice, dropped a couple of tones when he was speaking with her. It sent little tingles through her mind and made a direct beeline for parts of her body that she would be embarrassed to tell her mother about. Corey had hit her "other" spot as well; every time they were together and the last time they were together he hit it so many times she lost count. She also liked the way he held her close when they hugged. His big arms wrapping around her and making her feel safe and warm. Especially when they cuddled. She felt very relaxed and at ease from the beginning with him. So with that and being smart, humorous and rich. No way was she letting this one get away without a real good reason.

“ What time”, she cooed into the phone in response to Corey’s question about drinks.

“ About 6:30 good”, I asked?

“ 6:30 is perfect babe.”

“ Alright. I’ll see you then”, I responded, blowing her a kiss as I hung up the phone.

“Bye”, Alexis nearly whispered.

“ Could you stop glowing please, you’re fucking up my light”, Katie said faking exasperation at the mushiness she had just witnessed with Alexis and Corey’s phone call.

“ You’re just jealous”, Alexis teased.

“ Hell yeah, I am”, Katie joked.

The two of them laughed

“ I don’t remember me saying anything when the incredible Enrique was ringing your bells, missy.”

“ Alrighty then. Changing subjects quickly”, Katie said and the two of them laughed again.

Enrique was Katie's on again, off again Venezuelan boyfriend. Currently traveling to various parts of the world doing systems integration for large computer companies.

" So what are you guys doing tonight?"

" We're going to the bar for drinks with Paul and Sophie.

" Sounds fun."

"Yes, it does", Alexis, added.

" Well let's get these last orders logged in, so you can be ready. I'm sure you don't want to keep Mr. Woodward waiting."

" Isn't that a woman's prerogative", Alexis said laughing.

" You are so bad", Katie said shaking her head.

" Let's get this stuff out of the way. I'll finish the manufacturing order, while you finish the billing"

Alexis sat down at her desk and grabbed a small stack of invoices.

An hour or so later, the guard called up from downstairs.

" Ms. Parkhurst, you have a visitor. Mr. Woodward", said the guard.

" I'll be right down, thanks", said Alexis, hanging up the phone.

" Your knight in shining armor has arrived in his trusty limo to whisk you away?"

" Yes, Madame. I will see you tomorrow. Don't stay here working like a madwoman. Get out and do something, OK!"

" Yada, yada, yada. Get out of here. I'll see you tomorrow", said Katie.

Alexis gave Katie a hug, grabbed her purse and headed for the door.

" Who knows? Maybe Enrique is back in town", she quipped.

Katie turned around, mouth ajar as Alexis quickly slipped out of the door, laughing.

"What a bitch", Katie said out loud, smiling. She was looking forward to a relaxing evening with friends and the bar sounded like the perfect place for a Sunday evening. Some drinks, finger food, maybe some pool.

The elevator arrived and transported Alexis to the first floor, once outside she looked around for the limousine, not spotting that she looked for the Maserati. Nothing.

Corey lowered the tinted passenger side, window of his car.

"Sorry, Lex. I forgot you didn't know this one", I said.

Alexis shook her head, and got into the vehicle, when Corey opened the door for her.

" Okay, so I know to never look for any particular vehicle now. How many cars do you have? Or should I even ask", she said smiling?

" Just this one, the Maserati, an Escalade and the Limo here, but I have about 14 all together. I lose count sometimes."

" I'm sure you do", Alexis countered sarcastically.

We pulled off and headed for the Chrysler expressway and our destination north to Royal Oak to meet with Paul and Sophie.

" So how was your day", I asked?

" Hectic, but that's a good thing and you?

" Very relaxing", I said slowly.

" You know. I'm going to start not liking you", she said smiling.

"What? What did I do?"

" Rubbing it in like that", she said.

" Who me", I said pretending to be innocent, but chuckling.

" Yes you", she said smiling.

" Rubbing it in, is what I intend to do to you when we get back to your place", I said placing my hand firmly on her inner thigh.

" Hmmm, hope the night goes quick", she said turning towards me and giving me a quick kiss on the cheek.

We arrived at the bar, in a few short moments. Found a parking space not far from the venue and walked the short distance to the club. This particular bar was a Bar and Pool Hall for the Suburban set. The first floor was filled with pool tables, two bars and a few small tables, but the second floor is where they had live entertainment and DJ's.

We headed for the second floor, as that would be where Paul and Sophie would know to meet us.

Before long they joined us and after all of the greetings were exchanged and with Sophie still looking a little "not in a great mood, we all ordered drinks and finger foods and got down to the main purpose of the day…whipping Paul's ass on the pool table, like I did on the golf course earlier.

" What do you guys play", Alexis asked?

" 8 ball, no slop", Paul said." You want to "lag" for the break, flip a coin, or what Corey", Paul inquired?

" You can go first my dude, might as well keep the same formula as the golf course today", I said with a sheepish grin.

Paul looked over with exasperation on his face.

" How did the game go today", Sophie asked?

" Corey said they had a great time, but that could mean anything with these two though", Alexis added and the women laughed.

"Ha ha, that's it. You are breaking Mr. " luckiest man alive"", Paul said.

" Thank you, old friend. Much obliged. I will try and keep this quick and painless", I quipped.

" Kind of like last night", Alexis joked as I lined up my shot.

Her and Sophie laughed as I feigned shock.

" No you did not just take it there…and with a straight face even", I replied standing up straight?

Both women laughed.

" I'm sorry baby. I was just kidding", Alexis said coming over to me, from the bar stool she was sitting on. She gave me a quick hug and kiss on the cheek, then returned to her seat

" You two seem to be getting pretty comfortable", Sophie, whispered to Alexis.

" I'm having a good time", Alexis admitted.

" Are you over there conspiring with the enemy", I said after noticing the two of them whispering.

“Not at all baby. Just a little girl talk”, said Alexis.

“ We were discussing your snoring”, Sophie added.

“ Hey! I don’t snore”, I complained.

All three of them looked at me with that, yeah right look. They all knew too, I thought, laughing to myself.

“ Ok. Only when I am really tired”, I finally admitted.

I was beginning to like this thing with Alexis, a lot. Our dry senses of humor matched perfectly and she was a very fun woman to be around.

Maybe even to the point of it becoming something permanent. As I leaned over to take my shot, I glanced over at Alexis. Smiling; laughing; when she noticed me looking, she stuck her tongue out like a child and we both chuckled slightly at the silliness of her gesture. Yes, I thought. I’m beginning to really like this.

I took my shot, sending all of the pool balls scattering around the table. As they began to slow and settle, the 5 ball drifted its way into the side pocket and the 2 into the left corner.
" The beginning of a beautiful night", I said lining up for my next shot.
" Bartender, another round please", Paul said, easing onto a barstool.

CHAPTER XVIV

Monday morning came and Amanda feeling even worse than before immediately made an appointment with her physician. She had enlisted her friend Melissa to go with her, as she was feeling light headed. It was a short wait in the reception area, before the doctor was able to see her and Melissa busied herself with magazines and talk shows.

" So what seems to be the problem, Mandy", asked Dr. Steiner?

Dr. Marc Steiner had been the family physician for years. Had treated her parents, her and Corey since they were teenagers.

In his mid 50's, with a solid fatherly build, salt and pepper hair with matching beard and mustache. Amanda always felt calm when she had to come see him.

" I've had a shortness of breath, dizziness and some aches and pains. It has been really difficult at times to walk and a few days ago, I spit up a little blood."

" You spit up blood?"

"Yes."

" Unless you know the source, like a tooth or something like that, you should immediately call a doctor if you spit up blood, Amanda. You don't want to take any chances."

" I figured I would be okay, until today, I had no additional episodes."

" Well, let's get you checked out. I'm going to run a few tests and would like to take an ex-ray before you leave."

" Alright."

" I'll be right back."

After a few moments, the nurse returned with an examination gown.

"Hey Mandy. Not doing good today huh", she asked?

" No. I haven't been feeling like me for a few days now. Something had to have happened on my vacation in Florida."

" Well, we will get you all checked out and get you back on the road. Could you change into this and the doc will be back in just a few moments."

" Okay. Thanks Sara", I said and took the gown she offered.

Disrobing down to her underwear, Amanda now noticed the slight bruise on her left side in the brighter light of the examination office. Whatever it was, it definitely had something to do with the accident in Florida. Now she was sure.

After a few moments the doctor returned. Took her temperature and blood pressure, examined the bruise on her side and then sent her for X-rays.

The nurse escorted her down the long, cold corridor to the x-ray room, where she sat and waited for the technician to come in. It seemed like forever as she sat there, cold, in the dimly lit room.

The technician finally arrived and instructed her in the stances he would like to take the x-ray photos in.

After, taking several "shots", Alexis waited again for the nurse to return and take her back to the examination room.

" You guys really ought to consider some space heaters in here", Amanda said as Sara opened the door.

" Tell me about it. You should try working here", Sara said smiling.

Amanda smiled and followed her out of the room into the hallway again.

" You know the routine miss. Doc will be right in, in a few moments", Sara said ushering me into the exam room again.

Dr. Steiner entered the examination room, carrying the x-rays, about 20 minutes later. The look on his face was one of seriousness. Walking over to a light box against one wall, he hung the x-ray photos up and turned on the apparatus. Shining light through the film, so as to show me what they had discovered. He then sat on his stool, adjusted his glasses and looked at me.

" Amanda, you have a serious situation. Apparently you have a bone that has been splintered from your ribs. That splinter has scratched one of your kidneys, which accounts for the blood that you expelled."

" A bone from my ribs has cut my kidney?"

" A scratch. However that bone could become more dislodged. It could turn into a full fracture; it could puncture your kidney… It's not something that we should leave to heal. It's something that we should operate on and remove", he said.

" Oh my God", Amanda exclaimed!

" I would like to schedule as soon as possible."

" Doctor Steiner, I, I uhm", Amanda stammered.

" I understand Amanda, it is a big situation and it can easily turn into a much bigger situation if left unattended."

" I need to absorb this Doctor Steiner."

" You don't have a lot of time Amanda and there are no better choices."

" I will call you tomorrow Doctor Steiner. I just, I just need to think for a minute", Amanda said.

" Don't take too long Amanda and whatever you do be very careful. As I said that splinter could easily turn into a full fracture and it could wind up puncturing your kidney from where it is sitting."

" I understand."

" I really would like to admit you to the hospital right now…"

" Dr. Steiner, I just need to go home, for a minute. Just a little while and get my…get my everything in order, please", Amanda queried. Dr. Steiner sighed.

" Call me Tomorrow, Amanda and be very careful", Dr. Steiner said in a fatherly tone

" I will", she replied.

" Alright. In the meantime I'm going to give you something for the pain and that will help you sleep tonight and you contact me tomorrow. We'll get you set up and take care of this problem."

" Thank you Doc."

" I'll send Sara back with your lollipops", He said smiling.

Amanda smiled as well and laughed a little. Doctor Steiner remembered how, even as a 13-year-old, brat, she was always a good girl to get her lollipops from him when her mother brought her to the doctor. He did it to remind her that he has always been there for her.

It worked to make her feel at ease. Even though she was still slightly distraught about the situation.

She was not looking forward to any type of operation, as if anyone ever is.

CHAPTER XX

Time stood still and sped up simultaneously for Alexis and I. Every day was like entering into a new adventure. My restaurant and nightclub was reviewed in several magazines and after our opening night concerts was noted as "The" new hotspot on the streets. Alexis had sold out of her Spring/summer inventory and soon advertising would start for her fall/winter line. In the meantime, we had each other as major distractions to the happenings of the world.

From shopping, to romantic walks in the park and along the promenade by her apartment, overlooking the Detroit river, to spending quality cuddle time watching old movies and throwing popcorn at each other, Alexis and I were bonding as if we had known each other for years.

In fact, we were so similar in our likes and dislikes that it truly began to feel like we were simply made for each other, that a higher power had guided our destiny to meet.

" What are you thinking", she asked, as I sat against a tree, with Alexis, sitting between my legs and leaning against my chest.

" I was thinking am I more hungry or more sleepy", I replied, smelling the bar-b-que grilling upwind of where we sat.

" Feeling a little lazy, are we?"

"Feeling relaxed and content and don't want to move from where I am."

" I'll make you a plate if you're hungry baby", she said.

"Mmmm, spoken like a true southern belle", I said.

" I may be an independent woman, but I'm traditional still in a lot of ways. I still like to take care of my man", she said.

" Are we calling me, your man now", I joked.

" Whatever, Big head", she said getting up.

"You're the closest thing to it, at this moment."

" Oh, don't get me wrong. I'm not mad at it at all. In fact, it kind of has a nice ring to it", I replied.

"What do you want?"

"Other than your sexy ass, let's see…uhm, some ribs, macaroni & cheese and greens", I said.

" Desert…and don't say me either, smarty".

" I wasn't going to say me, I was going to say you though", I laughed.

"You are so stupid sometimes", she said.

" Maybe some apple or sweet potato pie."

" Ok. I'll be right back", she said.

" Thank you baby."

I watched as Alexis walked over to the food tent, where Grill king had set up.

I loved the way Alexis walked. Her hips swaying seductively as she moved.

This picnic was an annual event that I put on for networking with other promoters and artists.

My family members and friends from back in the day all showed up for this event every year. Now Alexis was the completion of the circle. At least that was how she was starting to make me feel. Especially since out of the five years that I had been doing this, I always seemed to be "out" of a relationship when this time came around. Sure I had bought dates a couple of times, but Alexis felt like more than just a date. We were not officially a couple, but I had figuratively locked my little black book away, after the first week of us dating. The two of us had been spending every day and night together and now we were adding even more friends and family that was witnessing our feelings blossom.

Alexis came back to where I sat with a plate and a can of soda and sat next to me.

I took the plate and fork she offered, said a silent prayer and placed the fork into the macaroni & cheese. Macaroni and cheese and the sauce on the Bar-b-que were always the true test of soul food. If those were good, then it was likely that everything else would be good as well. I placed the first bite in my mouth, savoring the taste.

“Mmmm, I love food from Grill King. They are the best”, I said.

“ This is a good event that you put on Corey.”

“Thank you. Just my way of keeping everybody close and working together”, I said placing the fork into the macaroni again. I bought the fork up close to Alexis’ lips. She opened her mouth and took the bite from the fork.

“Delicious. You just might be right about them”, Alexis said after swallowing the macaroni I offered her.

I finished eating, sharing my food with her and then we decided to go for a walk through the park.

We walked holding her hands as we passed by the baseball diamond and watched the children playing and the boats cruising along the river. Alexis turned to me, with a serious expression on her face.

" In case it is not obvious, I'm falling for you, Corey Woodward", she said.

I wasn't quite sure what to say. The feeling was of course mutual, but it just kind of came out of left field to hear her say it like that.

" I was a goner the day we met", I finally said.

She smiled.

Alexis stopped walking and pulled me close to her. Gently placing her hands on the side of my head, she kissed me very tenderly, and then looked me directly in my eyes.

" I'm a little afraid of how I am starting to feel about you. Actually, I've been feeling it for a little while now, I just wanted to get to know you and I wanted to be cautious and practical."

" Love is not practical baby. It comes and it is undeniable, no matter how much we want to pretend it is not there, but it is very fragile. It will leave if it is not nurtured."

" You used the word, love", she said looking at me.

" Yes, I did. I love you Alexis."

Alexis melted into my arms, squeezing me tightly as if she was never going to let me go. She kissed my neck, my ear lobe, and my cheek and then came around taking my face into her hands and kissed me passionately on the lips.

" I Love you", she said.

I returned her kisses, our passion rising.

" I can't wait to get you home", I said.

Her hands traced my body down the sides, as we kissed. She gripped my behind, before sliding her hand to the front of my pants. Feeling me erect and throbbing.

" Who said you have to wait", she said smiling and pushing me behind a patch of bushes?

CHAPTER XXI

Corey met with Amanda for lunch. She had said it was extremely important and she didn't sound like her usual self when she said it. She sounded scared.

I wasn't sure what fresh hell, Amanda could be going through, but at the end of the day. This was my sister and I loved her dearly.

Amanda was already there waiting for me, once I entered the restaurant, I greeted her with a kiss on the cheek and we sat at the table

" So what's going on Manda bear", I said calling her the nickname I had used since we were kids.

Amanda looked away briefly and lowered her head.

" Did you have a good day Corey", she asked, changing the subject for a moment.

I knew my sister and her stalling like that was a sure sign that something was seriously out of wack.

“ It was fine Manda, but what’s wrong? I can see it in your face.”

“ Corey, I’m sorry that I wasn’t able to come to your grand opening days.”

That made two times that she had redirected the conversation.

Now she was starting to scare me.

“ I might open a couple more in the future. There will be others”, I said trying to wait for her to feel comfortable.

“ Maybe, not for me”, she said.

“ What are you talking about?”

“ Corey, I went to see Dr. Steiner last week. While I was in Florida, a wave came in suddenly and pushed me against the reef.”

“ Yes”, I said turning anxious.

“ I’ve been bleeding internally a little. They want me to have an operation. Immediately.”

“Immediately! Then what the hell are we doing in this restaurant Amanda”, I asked concerned?

“ Immediately as within a day or so. I’m headed home to take care of a few things, grab some stuff and then I’m checking into the hospital in a couple of hours”, she said.

“ Today?”

“ Yes, They wanted me there last week, but I couldn’t do it. I was too nervous and scared and wanted a second opinion. I thought things would change, but they have only gotten worse this week. I will be checking in at Harrison hospital. I’m nervous Corey”, she said and leaned over, taking my hands in hers.

I pressed my forehead against hers, like we used to do when we told each other secrets, when we were kids.

“ I will be there Amanda. It’s all going to be okay.”

“ So what are they saying the bleeding is from?”

“ A fractured bone has scratched my kidney. It hasn’t punctured it, but if they don’t repair it, it could.”

She reached up to touch my cheek and kissed me on the forehead.

I knew she was scared and I was going to be there for my sister.

" I love you Corey", she said.

" I love you Manda bear", we stood up and hugged each other tightly.

" I have to stop by the house and then I am going to the hospital…"

" I'll meet you there, or call me when you get there", I said.

We walked out of the restaurant. Completely forgetting about ordering lunch and I walked her to her car. I needed to absorb all of what Amanda had just told me.

Amanda pulled off and I left to go to my car. I wasn't sure what to think at this point. I just wanted her to be okay and I was upset with myself for being angry with her about my grand opening. She and I were all each other had as far as immediate family. My sister had always been somewhat of an elusive, strong minded individual, and there were definite times that I felt she had not been there for me, the way I felt a sister should have been. Despite all of those feelings, she was my sister. My only sister and I truly loved her deeply. A bond that only blood could create. I was supposed to meet up with Alexis after this. I told her I had a luncheon appointment, but when I called her, her phone just rang, until voicemail picked up.

“ Hey babe. I’m downtown. Hit me up when you get this message”, I said, and then hung up.

Where to go now, I thought. I went back into the restaurant and ordered a drink. I needed to sort through the information that Amanda had just given me. Scratched kidney, potential punctures, this was a serious situation and then it dawned on me how dangerous the situation could be.

I tried dialing Alexis again, but still received no answer. She must be tied up I thought, I might as well head home and wait for Amanda to call me to meet her at the hospital.

I waited another 15 minutes, while I finished my drink and then dialed Alexis once more. " Hey sexy, you must be tied up. I'm going to run back to my place for a minute and then I have something to do later, but get a hold of me when you get a chance. Miss you", I said into the phone and then hung up.

I paid the bar tab and left. Walking past the restaurants and bars; People going about their daily business as I headed for my car.

Amanda was going to be just fine, I thought to myself. There was no need to panic.

I'll head home, change clothes and probably by then Alexis would be free of whatever was holding her up. I needed to tell her about Amanda and the hospital. Maybe we would be able to hook up later tonight. I walked around to the other side of the hotel where the restaurant was located, over to the valet and where I had left my car. I gave the numbered ticket to the valet that greeted me and he went to get my car.

I wondered why Alexis was not answering her phone. She was exactly like me in the effect that her phone was attached at the hip and very rarely would she not answer it.

They say that when it rains it pours, and with the situation that Amanda just laid on me, I was praying that it was not the case this time.

The Valet pulled my car up to the door and got out, with the engine running and the door open.

“Thanks”, I said handing him a tip.

“ Thank you sir”, he replied.

I got in, exiting the hotel and pulling into the Jefferson avenue afternoon traffic.

I needed to make this quick and get to the hospital and these Detroit streets were not going to hold me captive today.

CHAPTER XXII

I made it back to my place and Alexis finally returned my calls. Within a few moments, Alexis and I stood in the atrium of my house. She had asked if she could stop by for a moment to talk. Today was a little unusual though, because I normally would have heard from her by now and it was almost 3pm, when I finally did talk to her.

When I had called her earlier, my phone messages had gone unanswered and then she wanted to stop by. I hoped nothing weird had gone on in her day, but something in her voice wasn't exactly right and in my present state of condition, I didn't have the strength to figure it out. I told her, of course she could come by, and within a few moments she made it to my door.

" Hey boo", I said as she entered and leaned over to give her a kiss.

" Hi Corey", she said moving away from me.

" What's wrong", I asked?

"Corey, I think that we need to take a break from each other", she started.

" What? What's wrong? What happened?"

It was just yesterday that we had told each other that we were in love. What could have happened in 24 hours, I wondered. This had to be some sort of cold feet or nervousness.

" My feelings for you have grown rather rapidly and I don't think we are in the same mind state. So, I think it best for us to cool it for a while."

" What are you talking about? I thought we were doing okay and my feelings for you have also grown quickly. We just admitted that yesterday"

" I wish I could believe yesterday."

" Why can't you believe it?"

" Corey, dammit! I wish you would stop playing this little game with me. I saw you and the girl that you are seeing downtown, we just need to break this off and go on about our separate ways."

"What girl? I'm not seeing anybody", I asked, thoroughly confused.

" Look, even though you were the only person that I was seeing, we didn't have any official commitment Corey. There was no need for you to be sneaking around like a child. You could have been an adult about it, if you wanted to see someone else."

" You're right there is no reason for me to sneak around…"

" Was!"

" Alexis I wasn't sneaking around doing anything…"

" You could have fooled me. So who is this tramp that you have to be all hugged up with, getting late night phone calls from and leaving all the time, all of a sudden?"

"Alexis…"

" You know what, it don't even matter. It don't even fucking matter", Alexis said as she headed for the door.

" Alexis, wait a minute", I said starting to get angry.

“ Wait for what? For you to conjure up some more lies?”

“ First off dammit, I am not lying to you and I never have.”

“ Goodbye Corey. Don’t fucking call me, don’t email me, text me, come by, nothing. You understand? Nothing”, Alexis said turning around and stomping towards the door.

“ Alexis, I am not seeing anyone else. Would you stop for a minute?”

Alexis kept walking, opened the door and left it swinging as she stepped out of it.

I thought about going after her, but then didn’t. I guess prior experiences and hurts, took over at that moment. Knowing that right now with her angry, she wasn’t going to hear anything or anybody.

As I headed for the kitchen, it dawned on me. She saw me hugging and kissing, Amanda. It had to be. That was the only woman that my lips have been near, other than Sophie since we met.

" Oh my God", I thought as I realized what had happened.

I wanted to run after her and straighten it out, but I knew that she was going to have to calm down a little first. This was fucked up. I have really started feeling very deep feelings for her and now she thinks I am lying to her and seeing another woman on the side. She mistook my sister, for another woman.

I sat down in the plush recliner in my living room. Forgetting about the kitchen altogether. Gripping my head with both hands. I needed to solve this. I thought about calling Sophie and maybe she could help straighten this mess out. As I reached for my cell phone, I paused, If Alexis didn't trust me, then we had nothing.

I was conflicted. This was something with a very simple and easy explanation, but what happens the next time?

I felt a sharp pain in my chest and closed my eyes tightly to choke back a tear, I felt forming at the edge of my eye.

It was that moment that I realized, that I wasn't just feeling strong feelings for her.
I was in love with her.
I needed to get down to the hospital.
Unfortunately this situation was going to have to wait and I couldn't believe that all of this was really happening to me, right now.
I got up and left through the garage entrance, grabbing the Maserati keys from the peg by the back door. Hitting the garage door opener as I started the car.
The engine, growled under the hood like a Panther that had just been startled awake.
When the garage door fully opened, I jammed it into gear and screeched out and onto the street. Headed for Beaumont hospital.
Approximately 20 minutes later, I pulled into the parking lot at Harrison Hospital and maneuvered into the closest space to the entrance. Hurrying into the building, not really knowing where I was going, thinking about what had just happened between Alexis and I, worried about my sister…all of these thoughts,

surely could be seen in my facial expressions as I walked up to the information counter.
" I'm looking for Amanda Woodward", I said to the attendant.
" Is she a patient or employee", she asked?
"Patient. She should have checked in, just recently."
The attendant checked into her computer, looking for Amanda's name.
" She is in emergency."
"Emergency", I said frantically?
" She was brought in about 20 minutes ago", the nurse said.
I bolted for the electronic doors. I only knew how to get to emergency from the outside and I wasn't in the mood to stand around waiting for directions. I ran to the other side of the building and into the admitting doors for the emergency area.
" Amanda Woodward, please", I said to the emergency attendant, breathlessly. " She's a patient, admitted about 20 minutes ago."

"Relative", she asked, typing the name into her computer?

" Yes. Her brother", I said.

"She has been admitted, they have taken her into surgery. Just a moment, I will have someone come out to speak with you."

The nurse picked up her phone and dialed an extension. Explaining who and what was going on to the party that answered. Within a few terse seconds she hung up. She is being prepped. Go straight down that hallway to the double doors, Dr. Steiner will meet you there and take you back to your sister."

"Thank you", I said and moved quickly down the corridor she indicated.

At the door, Dr. Steiner was waiting for me. I had not seen him in years. He was our family physician since Amanda and I were kids. At least with him there, I knew that he was going to do everything he could to help her.

"Hello, Dr. Steiner", I said, extending my hand to greet him.

" Hello, Corey. Mandy is being brought around to be taken up for surgery. She had a splintered bone, which progressed into a full fracture. A fragment of the bone was pressed near her kidney. That bone has now punctured it."

"Oh my God", I said lowering my head and attempting to hold it together.

A nurse and attendant wheeled into view, pushing a bed with Amanda on it.

"Manda", I said as I approached the bed

She turned towards me, slowly opening her eyes. I could tell she was in major pain.

"Corey."

" You're going to be just fine Manda Bear. I'm here. Dr. Steiner is here", I said, reassuring her and walking next to the bed and holding her hand.

" Corey, I was on my way here and I had to hit my brakes hard. The seat belt tightened and pulled against my side.

The next thing I knew there was just a really fucked up pain in my side and I blacked out. I woke up here", she told me.

" She is very fortunate that someone discovered her as quickly as they did" Dr. Steiner added.

We arrived at the surgery doors.

"Corey, I love you", she said.

"I love you too Manda", I said.

"Corey, I will come out as soon as we get her stabilized", Dr. Steiner assured me. Stopping me at the door.

I stood paralyzed mentally as Doctor Steiner turned and went into the operating room.

I watched as they went through the second set of swinging doors and then headed for the waiting room.

I sat down on one of the corner chairs, a mixed bag of emotions.

Alexis had mistaken my meeting with Amanda as me sneaking around on her and my sister was in an operating room fighting for her life.

It had been a long time since I felt this helpless and there was nothing I could do, but wait and pray.

It hurt, but Alexis would have to wait. That was a misunderstanding that ultimately had an answer and would be solved relatively simply. At least I sincerely hoped that it would.

Right now, I just needed Amanda to be okay. Needed Dr. Steiner to emerge from the operating room with a smile on his face and tell me that all was well.

I sat in the waiting room with every second ticking in my brain, my hands clasped, rocking in the chair.

CHAPTER XXIII

Alexis sat behind the wheel of her car, stunned in the parking lot of her building. Confused at what she had seen. Confused and upset at what she had just done.

What she saw was Corey and another woman in an intimate embrace. She was parked just opposite of a downtown hotel, on the side street and had seen Corey walk out with and then hug and kiss another woman. A million thoughts crossed her mind, Including thoughts of what she had done for him to not be satisfied, the thought that she had believed that Corey was different from the other men, from some of the men that had been in her life. That Corey was different from Lew, the last man to destroy her heart.

She was not going to let this one destroy her mind though. She had thought about confronting them right there and bitch slapping that hoe, but thought better of it at the last moment. If that was what he wanted to do, there was nothing that her or anyone else was going to be able to do to change it. There was nothing worse than two women fighting over a man, she thought to herself and she was not going to let this ruin her life and her career. Dammit, not this time.

She watched as the woman pulled off and Corey after a moment of watching her drive away, left, heading for the other side of the building.

A few minutes later she saw him pull off in his Lexus. He had tried to call her, but she couldn't bring herself to answer the phone. Not right then.

Fighting back tears, she put her Jag in gear and headed for her apartment, not understanding and wishing to God that she didn't trust her own eyes. It was for nothing though, because she did trust her own eyes and she knew what she saw. She and Corey had been growing so very close, they were together constantly, she thought for sure that what they were establishing was something that was going to last. She had thought the same thing with her Ex though and she was very, very tired of being fooled.

She was determined not to cry, but she was in denial. This hurt, even worse than with Lew. At least with him, she had a suspicion. She knew that Lew was a player, player and everyone had told her that he was foul. Corey was somebody everyone trusted and everyone confided in. This from Corey was a complete surprise.

She pulled onto Jefferson; just moments after he did, but continued towards the left and towards the apartment complex, while Corey had merged with traffic onto the Lodge freeway to the right.

Alexis tried not to speed, she tried not to cry, but it was inevitable. As she pulled in between the gates where residents swiped their electronic gate keys, the tears began to fall. She made it to her parking space, still trying to choke them back, and exited the vehicle.

She lost her war with her tears as she stepped onto the elevator to take her upstairs to her living quarters. She began to cry uncontrollably, her breaths short.

The elevator ride, although very swift, seemed to take forever and as she reached her floor, she bolted for her apartment.

The remainder of her emotions spilled from her body as she closed the door behind her. Closed the door to the outside world, where only her own four walls could bear witness to her pain. The four walls and Katie.

"Alexis", Katie said surprised and rushed to the doorway, just as Alexis collapsed to the floor. " What's wrong? What happened", she asked.

Alexis buried her face into her friends shoulder.

"Corey is cheating on me!"

"What? Are you sure Lex? Tell me what happened." She asked

" I had parked on the side of a hotel downtown near Jefferson. As I sat there getting ready to turn the ignition key, I saw Corey and another woman emerge from the hotel. They hugged and she saw them Kiss, before she got into her car and Corey left to go get his car."

"What", Katie exclaimed?

" I went to his house and broke it off with him. I can't take this shit Katie. Every time I get close to someone, they hurt me like this", she said."

"Alexis, it will be okay", Katie said moving forward and putting her arms around her friend.

Alexis held her tightly and released even more of her tears.

"Lex, I'm really shocked. Corey doesn't seem like that type of person. There has got to be some sort of explanation to all of this."

Katie had obviously not known Corey very long, but something just didn't seem right. He didn't seem to be that type of man.

" I saw what I saw, Katie. How am I going to deny that?"

Alexis had not even considered that she could have been wrong. She had allowed the situation to affect her immediately and had made a decision in order to protect her heart. No, she couldn't be wrong. She wouldn't even allow herself to think that way. She couldn't.

" What did you say when you got to his house? You broke it off? What kind of explanation did he give you?"

" I didn't even allow him to conjure up any lies."

" Alexis! You didn't even give him a chance to explain the situation?"

"No."

" Oh my God, baby", Katie said. Wrapping her arms around her friend as she began to cry even more. On one hand she hoped Alexis was right in her decision, because if she wasn't she had just let go of a man that truly seemed to love her. On the other hand she hoped she was wrong and that there would be some way to straighten this whole mess out, before it really became too late.

" Shh, it will be okay Lex", she said rubbing her back.

" Why do I always have to go through this? Why can't I find someone that just wants to be with me and me alone?"

" Lex, I think we all have asked ourselves that question at one time or another. You just have to do your best and roll with the frogs until the prince actually shows up."

" That is so fucked up", Alexis said laughing at the irony and trying to wipe the tears from her eyes.

" Something just isn't right here though Lex. Corey just doesn't seem like that type.

" I didn't think so either, but what am I to think?"

" I think the situation with Lew has you on such pins and needles that you didn't give the man the chance to explain is what I think. I don't know whether to hope you're right on this or to hope that you are wrong. I just know it doesn't feel right", Katie said.

Alexis thought for a moment, hoping that she had not reacted rashly and then dismissed the thought. She knew what she saw.

CHAPTER XXIV

I dialed Paul and he picked up on the first ring.
" What's popping Corey", he said?
"Paul, I'm at Harrison hospital. Amanda is about to have an emergency surgery", I said attempting not to choke up on the phone.
" We'll be right there Corey", Paul said without any hesitation or asking me what was wrong.
We both hung up and I leaned back into the chair.
If there was anybody that I could count on in this world, it was Paul. We had been friends through the roughest parts of life since childhood and were still the best of friends now.
A few minutes later Paul and Sophie arrived at the hospital. Sophie and Paul both came up and hugged me.
" We got here as soon as we could. What happened", Paul asked?

" Amanda was pushed against a reef while she was in Florida. The impact injured her ribs and splintered a bone that had been pressed against her kidney. On her way here, she hit her brakes hard and the seatbelt injured the bone further and punctured her kidney."

" Oh my God", Sophie said.

"They wheeled her into surgery just before I called you."

" It's going to be okay", Paul, said pulling my head into his shoulders, hugging me.

" Let's go sit down", Sophie suggested and we all moved back towards the waiting area.

" Where is Alexis", Sophie asked?

" I don't know. She broke up with me", I said.

"What!"

"What are you talking about", Sophie asked?

" Apparently, she was somewhere downtown when Amanda and I met up and saw me kiss her goodbye. She mistook Amanda for some woman I was seeing as well as her and accused me of sneaking around, when I could have just been adult about it."

At this point it was getting very hard to maintain my composure and a single tear rolled from my eye. I breathed in deeply, containing the emotions racing through my mind and body. Sophie wrapped her arms around me.

"Oh my God! Corey, I am so sorry. It's all a big misunderstanding though. It can be worked out."

" I'm not sure. If she is not going to trust me, we have nothing."

"Corey, this isn't the time, but remember I said Alexis had been through some very rough times? Her last seriously relationship ended because he was cheating on her", Paul reminded me.

" I'm not saying her reaction was justified, but she probably would not have reacted as quickly as she did if not for that. Give it a little time. It will straighten out."

" She has all the time in the world at this point", I said.

Paul and Sophie knew there was no use in talking about it further. It was going to be what it was going to be from this point forward, if we got back together or if we didn't get back together. Right now, my only concern was Amanda

The minutes began to feel like days as we sat there, waiting for her to be stabilized.

The three of us had been anxiously waiting for two and a half hours and at this point I was seriously starting to worry. At just the moment Sophie placed her hand on my back, Doctor Steiner emerged from the operating room. He was walking steadily, unsmiling, and took a very deep breath as he approached us. He lowered his head and placed his hand on my shoulder.

"She didn't make it…"

Nothing he said after that or anyone else for that matter, registered as my mind shut completely off. The wall of tears I had been holding in, burst through my mental dam and I could feel my vocal cords screaming, but no sound came out other than the choked, muffled moans from my throat as I fell to my knees. My sister was gone and in the blink of an eye, I was alone.

We had just held each other. We had finally come to grips and expressed how we really felt about each other at the restaurant. I had told her I would be there for her and that everything would be okay. It was not okay. It was not going to be okay.

Paul, Sophie and Dr. Steiner tried to lift me from the floor and into a chair.

As I fell back into the waiting room chair, I could feel my body shutting down and the muscles in my stomach beginning to cramp. I screamed, but there was no sound that escaped my throat.

CHAPTER XXV

It took three days for Sophie to catch up with Alexis. She left for Santa Monica and wasn't accepting any calls and wouldn't return calls to the office where Katie was.

Of course by now, Katie knew what had transpired and she frantically tried to get hold of Alexis herself, all without success.

Alexis finally showed back up in Detroit at her apartment and Katie grabbed her and hugged her the minute she hit the door.

" Where the hell have you been? We've been trying to get hold of you like crazy."

" To tell you the truth after the thing with Corey, I just didn't want to talk to anybody. I turned the phone off and just hibernated for a few days."

The security guard called up right at that moment and Katie grabbed the phone. It was Sophie. She told the guard to let her in and hung up the receiver.

" Lex, you had better sit down. I have something to tell you and it is not going to be easy or pretty", Katie said.

" What?"

" Hold on, let's wait on Sophie."

" What's going on", Alexis said sitting on the arm of the couch.

" Alexis, you are not going to be very happy…"

" I'm not happy already, what's new?"

" No. You are not going to be very happy with yourself."

The buzzer rang and Katie went to open the door for Sophie. She walked into the living room and saw Alexis.

" Bitch, where have you been", She said letting out an exaggerated breath.

" Sorry Soph. I just needed to get my head back together. Still not there, but, I gotta do what I gotta do."

Sophie turned to Katie.

"You haven't told her yet?"

" She just got here, I waited until you got up here."

" Tell me what? What's going on?"

" Oh, Lexis. You might need a drink", Sophie said.

Katie and Sophie sat down with Alexis and explained the entire situation to her.

Explaining that in fact Corey did have a sister and it was not just a cover up for a chick on the side. They explained that, the woman she saw at the hotel with Corey was in fact, Amanda and that on that very day, she had went to the hospital and wound up having emergency surgery. She died that day, due to her injuries.

Upon hearing the last part, Alexis, who had covered her wide opened mouth with her hands, burst into tears and looked as if she were going to have a seizure.

"Oh my God! Oh my God", she exclaimed over and over." What have I done?"

Sophie and Katie both wrapped their arms around her, attempting to console her.

She had done something to hurt the man that she was in love with. She had hurt the man that was truly in love with her and who had needed her.

“He’s never going to talk to me ever again”, Alexis said through tears. “ And I couldn’t blame him if he despised me for the rest of his life.”

“ Shh, Lex. The only thing you can do is to try girl. If there is any chance of fixing this, you have to take it.”

The two women held their friend close, until her tears subsided and her breathing had calmed down somewhat.

Alexis knew what she had to do and if she had to beg his forgiveness, this time, it was what she was going to have to do.

CHAPTER XXVI

I spent several days at my house, keeping myself busy after the misunderstanding and break up between Alexis and I. Between that and Amanda's death; I had been pretty much a wreck. I was a cautionary tale for all those who unfortunately came across me. Paul and Sophie had been there to support me. Trying to get me back into the swing of things, but I needed time to adjust to everything.

I wasn't motivated to do anything, to go anywhere. Sometimes even to eat.

Kenny was handling the club fantastically and my onsite managers handled all of my real estate concerns. In that respect I was very, very fortunate. Had I have had a 9 to 5 job, I would seriously be in trouble. I couldn't even imagine how someone in that position would deal with all of this without becoming very bitter, without losing their grip and/or getting fired because they couldn't perform their job for constantly thinking of their plight and pain. My relationship with Alexis had burned white hot as well, but I should have realized maybe that anything that hot would burn out quickly. At least that was the analogy I tried to console myself with. Ultimately, I thought, Alexis had been too perfect for me. A man wants to have a woman that is a ride or die chick. A woman kind of like his mother, but just not enough like his mother. A lady in the streets, and a whore in the sheets, as the cliché went or whatever it was. Alexis was all of that and more. Everything he had ever wanted in a woman. Mentally, I considered her an equal. A go-getter, such as myself. A person that could come up with an idea and follow that dream into making it a reality. I often wondered at the "others" in this world. The ones that always had the phrase, "stop dreaming" sprouting from their lips. Did they not realize that everything around them. Everything they touched, tasted, used on a daily basis, was once a dream in someone's head?

The clothes they wore, the car they drove, and the house they lived in on the street, in the city or country. All of those things were at one time, merely a dream. Often a dream that someone said to that person, quit dreaming. Sexually, we were compatible as well. At my age and through my experiences, I was not someone that would be described as a prude. Alexis was adventurous, giving and was not afraid to take as well. She knew what excited her and what pleased her and was not afraid or shy about sharing that information with her partner. She did it in a way also that would not make it seem as if she was unsatisfied, but merely looking to share and explore the next level of sexuality.

Physically, everything about her turned me on. From the shape of her feet to how her ankles connected to her long smooth legs and thick, muscular thighs. The shape of her ass and the way it contoured to her small waist and stomach muscles.

Her eyes, lips, nose, hair, lips…every small detail of her that I had taken in and etched across my memory. I couldn't even think of her sometimes without getting an erection. Then there was the most important aspect of Alexis Parkhurst. Her heart. She had to be one of the most caring persons that I had ever met. She also knew how to keep it thorough with me as opposed to the "Keep it real" manifesto just being a cliché or an excuse to say things that were potentially hurtful, but in our thing we call society was not supposed to hurt as long as we were honest about it. She did things, like when we woke up in the morning and hadn't had a chance to escape each other and freshen up, like tell me my breath stank and kiss me anyway. When I came back from running, not really expecting her and came into my house all sweaty from the jog, she pressed her body against me anyway. To look at her, you would think she would be a pampered little princess, but Alexis was real. Unlike a lot of women in this world, that was too busy worrying about their own lives to be able to truthfully include anyone else into their plans. I used to write poetry, songs and short stories, but had let those things fall away, as I got deeper into my career. The thing a lot of creative people fall victim to. Alexis had inspired me to write once again though. I had written a poem that I now kept on my mantle. I didn't know if it was to remind me of Alexis, down the line or to remind me that I was human and that somewhere out there on this cynical, messed up planet. There was someone out there that could make me feel these thoughts. Someone that could make my heart pulse, just a little bit faster at the mere thought of them. I thought about the words in that poem as I sat on my porch, enjoying the wind blowing across my face and the sound of birds chirping close by.

SHANNON W. BLOOMFIELD

If I were a Ship, I would have no sail...

A storm with no wind, an ocean with no end.

If I were a morning there would be no sun.

An evening with moon and stars, seen by no one.

If I were a rainbow, several colors would be missing...

perfect lips that have never experienced kissing.

If I were a path, I would lead nowhere...

Space with no air, Two of a kind, but still no pair...

A flower with no fragrance or scent...

anger with nowhere to vent.

I AM INCOMPLETE WITHOUT YOU.

If I were a car, I would have no gas,

no wheels and no seat...

A fresh field of apples with no one to eat.

If I were a dream, I would have no beginning

or end...

A dry martini without Vodka or Gin

If I were a beach, there would be no sand

and in the brightest sun, no one would tan.

If I were still a child

I would never have experienced a smile

never differentiated between sadness or joy,

A Christmas day with no toy.

I AM INCOMPLETE WITHOUT YOU

If I were evil, there would be no sin

A good man with no love and no friend.

If I were a fish, I would not swim

A room brightly lit, but somehow dim

I would be a man, but still not a father,

without Love or God, why would I bother

If I were a time I would not exist...

and if we never met... You'd still be missed...

As I ran all of these thoughts through my mind, a silver Jaguar pulled in front of my house. At first I was off guard, wondering whom it could be, but then as I turned around, I realized that it was Alexis.

Parking her car, stepping out and then coming up my driveway. Slowly walking toward the front entrance, where I was standing. My heart was pounding, I had not seen her for weeks at this point and wondered if I was to ever see her again. It had all been a misunderstanding.

" Hi", she said when she finally reached me.

I looked at her. Not really knowing what to say. I took a deep breath and greeted her with a very dry hello. Even though my heart was screaming and my insides were turning over.

I wanted to just grab her, pull her close to me and tell her it was ok, but the fact of the matter is that it was not in my hands anymore. At least in my mind. Knowing the dynamic of men and women these days, it was probably never in my hands. In addition, I wasn't exactly sure, why she was here in the first place.

" I realize that you may not want to talk to me, right now and I would understand, but I couldn't stay away and not say something."

" I'm listening", I replied.

" I, uh, first want to apologize to you. I should have trusted you more. It's just that I was trying to protect my heart and unfortunately my past has me jumping the gun sometimes. Pulling the plug, when I should listen and try to work things out. Especially in this case."

" That is a two way street. I would have asked you", I said.

I knew that Sophie had informed her of everything that happened that last day we saw each other and that she had heard of my sister's death.

" I understand Corey and I am truly sorry."

Invariably we as humans do things everyday that cause questions or heartache to other people that we have no idea or clue as to how we are affecting them.

The problem is, is that people are so guarded and normally stressed from everyday living that they sometimes put on a deflective attitude if anyone were to question their actions or motives. The unfortunate part about that is that if a person is asking you about something, 9 times out of 10, they are trying to clarify a situation instead of just jumping to conclusions. A lot of us, have been conditioned that “How dare someone”, question our credibility or actions, when, in this society we live in, they would be a fool NOT to question you or anyone else for that matter. Women, especially who have had to “answer” to a man for this or that reason, have a huge chip on their shoulder. Especially if they are single and someone asks them about something they are doing or have done. You can almost hear the “I do what I want” attitude coming a mile away. So you have two choices. You either ask the person point blank about whatever it is that you want to know and risk the chance on losing them, causing an argument or alienating your relationship or you walk away, not knowing if it was something innocent and/or explainable or last, but not least keep it all inside and let it build until it blows up.

"In this particular case, you assumed that I was cheating on you and it never crossed your mind that the woman you saw me with, was my sister. Let alone the fact that she was not well."

" Corey, I am so very, very sorry, for not trusting you. I am very deeply in love with you and the feeling just won't stop. It won't go away. I can't go back to the way I was, dealing with the ones I can live with, I want to be with the man I can't live without and that is you."

I took a deep breath.

" Alexis, I'm not trying to have you uncomfortable or apologizing and shit. I am hurt by the distrust still at this very moment, but I would be lying not only to you, but also to myself if I said I didn't miss you and want to work through this. It's not something that we can't work through and in case you are not sure. I love you very much."

Those were not just words to me. As difficult as the situation was and offended by the trust issue, everyone makes mistakes. I knew I loved Alexis. I knew I wanted her. To not give it at least a chance in my mind would be a crime.

" Could you kiss me, before anything else happens", she asked moving closer to me.

I took her into my arms and kissed her as if there would never be another sunset or sunrise.

" Corey…I missed you so badly. I'm sorry baby. If I have to, I will spend the rest of my life making it up to you."

" I might hold you to that Miss Parkhurst", I said looking into her eyes." I love you Alexis."

" I love you", she returned.

" I'm just as much if not more so at fault. I was just so stunned by my sister's illness and then death. So overcome and not really knowing what to do", I said. " I just got so caught up in everything that it was all that occupied my mind for a moment and then when I reached out to you to explain, that is when everything went awry."

" Shh, baby", Alexis, said putting a finger to my lips. That is in the past and we have resolved the misunderstanding for now. Only thing that matters to me now is that we are together, we work this out and I don't ever want to lose you again."

She was correct, there was nothing else that mattered to me either after that except our kiss and us being together. No amount of money, no power and no obstacle is as important as when you find… true love.

DVD AND SOUNDTRACK

COMING SOON

www.myspace.com/westbloomfieldmovie

www.westbloomfieldmovie.com

www.Myspace.com/moderntribecommunications

www.Moderntribecommunications.com

www.ingramcontent.com/pod-product-compliance
Lightning Source LLC
LaVergne TN
LVHW050619100826
845148LV00011B/1656

* 9 7 8 0 5 7 8 0 1 7 9 5 2 *